"Teacher!" Sarah gushed. "How we missed you yesterday!"

"*Guder mariye,*" I[...] very glad to see yo[...] books at your des[...] the bell is rung."

"*Guder mariye,* Ha[...] [...]yer said as the children cantered out the door. "How are you?"

"I am glad to be back at school," she admitted. Then, with a faraway note in her voice, she said, "I'm glad the *kinner* are coming home with me today. I truly missed their presence yesterday. Without them, I felt… I don't know. I guess I might say I was at a loss."

Sawyer was flooded with a sense of warmth. "I was concerned your *groossdaadi* might not have wanted you to care for the *kinner* any longer," he ventured. "I didn't know what I would have done without you."

Hannah scrunched her eyebrows together. "Didn't Doris take *gut* care of them?"

"*Jah,* she did," Sawyer replied. "It's just that she's not…"

When he didn't finish his sentence, Hannah inclined her head to meet his eyes. "She's not what?" she asked.

He leaned forward, so as not to be overheard. "She's not *you*."

Carrie Lighte lives in Massachusetts, where her neighbors include several Mennonite farming families. She loves traveling and first learned about Amish culture when she visited Lancaster County, Pennsylvania, as a young girl. When she isn't writing or reading, she enjoys baking bread, playing word games and hiking, but her all-time favorite activity is bodyboarding with her loved ones when the surf's up at Coast Guard Beach on Cape Cod.

Books by Carrie Lighte

Love Inspired

Amish Triplets for Christmas

Amish Triplets for Christmas

Carrie Lighte

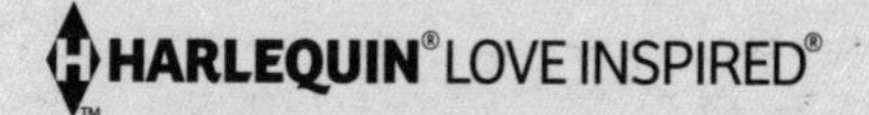

Recycling programs for this product may not exist in your area.

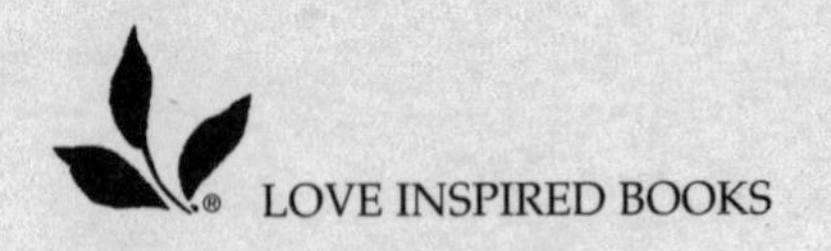

ISBN-13: 978-0-373-62316-7

Amish Triplets for Christmas

This edition published by arrangement with Love Inspired Books.

www.Harlequin.com

Printed in U.S.A.

And my God will meet all your needs according
to the riches of his glory in Christ Jesus.
—*Philippians* 4:19

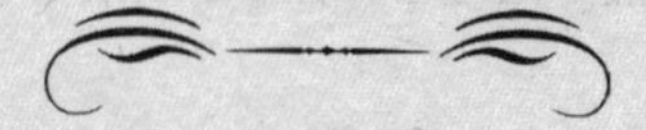

To my family,
who always supports my creative endeavors,
with thanks also to the Love Inspired team,
especially Shana Asaro,
for helping this dream become a reality.

Chapter One

Hannah Lantz rose from her desk, smoothed her skirt and forced her pale, delicate features into a smile. She didn't want the little ones to know how distraught she was that she would no longer be their teacher once harvest season ended. Positioning herself in the doorway, she waited to greet the scholars, as school-aged children were known, when they climbed the stairs of the two-room schoolhouse where she herself had been taught as a child.

Doris Hooley, the statuesque redheaded teacher who taught the upper-grade classes, stood on the landing, fanning herself with her hand. "It's so hot today, you probably wish Bishop Amos and the school board decided to combine your class with mine immediately instead of waiting until late October."

"Neh," Hannah replied, thinking about how desperately she and her grandfather needed the income she earned as a teacher. "I'm grateful they extended my position a little longer. It's been a blessing to teach for the past eleven years, and I'm truly going to miss the scholars."

"Jah," Doris agreed. "Such a shame so many young women from Willow Creek left when they married men from bigger towns in Lancaster County. Otherwise, enrollment wouldn't have dwindled. Not that I blame them. Willow Creek isn't exactly overflowing with suitable bachelors. That's why I'm so eager to meet John Plank's nephew

from Ohio. Not only is he a wealthy widower, but I've heard he's over six feet tall!"

Hannah cringed at her remarks. Thirty-six-year-old Doris never exercised much discretion about her desire to be married, a trait that eventually earned her the nickname of "Desperate Doris" within their small Pennsylvania district. As an unmarried woman of twenty-nine years herself, Hannah thought the term was mean-spirited, although if pressed, she had to admit it was fitting in Doris's case.

"I believe John's nephew is coming here to help with the harvest—not to meet a bride," Hannah contradicted as a cluster of children trod barefoot across the yard, swinging small coolers in their hands.

"That kind of pessimistic attitude is why you're still unmarried," Doris retorted, craning her neck to spy the first buggies rolling down the lane. "It isn't every day the Lord brings an eligible man to Willow Creek, and I, for one, intend to show him how *wilkom* he is here."

Hannah gave her slender shoulders a little shrug. "*I* intend to show his *kinner* how *wilkom* they are," she emphasized. "It can be difficult for young ones to start school in a new place. Besides, if it weren't for their increasing the size of my class, there would have been no need for the school board to keep me on. You could have managed the rest of my scholars yourself."

As the children approached, Hannah considered whether Doris was right. Was she being pessimistic about the prospect of marriage? Or was she merely accepting God's provision for her life? After all, she'd scarcely had any suitors when she was a teenager; her grandfather had seen to that. So what was the likelihood she'd find love in their diminishing district now, at this age?

Even if she did meet someone she wished to marry, her grandfather was incapable of living alone and too stubborn to move out of his house. She couldn't leave him, nor could she imagine any man being willing to live as her husband under her grandfather's roof and rule.

To her, it seemed only realistic to accept that no matter how much she may have yearned for it, her life wasn't meant to include the love of a husband. And she had come to believe God wanted her to be content with teaching other people's children rather than to be bitter about not having children of her own.

In any case, she figured she had more urgent priorities than pursuing a stranger who was only visiting their community—like figuring out what she'd do to support her grandfather and herself once her teaching position ended.

She shook her head to rid her mind of worrisome thoughts. *The Lord will provide*, she reminded herself. When Eli and Caleb Lapp said good-morning, a genuine smile replaced Hannah's forced one.

"Guder mariye," she returned their greeting enthusiastically as they clambered up the steps.

After all the older students were accounted for, Doris sighed. "I guess the wealthy widower isn't showing up today after all. Perhaps tomorrow."

She ducked into the building while Hannah waited for the final student to disembark her buggy. It was Abigail Stolzfus, daughter of Jacob Stolzfus, one of the few men Hannah had briefly walked out with when they were younger. But when he proposed to her almost nine years ago, she'd refused his offer.

"One day, your pretty face will turn to stone," he had taunted. "You'll end up a desperate spinster schoolmarm like Doris Hooley."

She knew Jacob's feelings had been hurt when he'd made those remarks, and she had long since forgiven his momentary cruelty. But this morning, she was surprised by how clearly his words rang fresh in her mind. Watching Jacob's daughter, Abigail, skip along the path to the schoolhouse, Hannah couldn't help but imagine what her life might have been like if she—instead of Miriam Troyer—had married him.

Granted, she never felt anything other than a sisterly fondness for Jacob, so a marriage to him would have been one of convenience only, which was unacceptable to her, even if her grandfather had permitted it. But might it have been preferable to being on the brink of poverty, as she was now? Thinking about it, she could feel the muscles in her neck tighten and her pulse race.

She chided herself to guard her thoughts against discontentment; otherwise, it would be her heart, not her face, that turned to stone. God had brought her through greater trials than losing her classroom. She trusted He must have something else in store for her now, too.

She reached out and patted Abigail on the shoulder, smiling reflexively when the child grinned up at her and presented a jar of strawberry preserves.

"*Denki*, Abigail. You know I have a weakness for strawberries!" she exclaimed, bending toward the girl. "Did you help your *mamm* make this?"

"Jah," Abigail replied. "I picked the berries, too."

"I will savor it with my sweet bread."

As the girl continued toward her desk, Hannah reached to shut the door behind her.

"Don't!" a deep voice commanded.

Startled, Hannah whirled around to find a tall sandy-haired man holding the door ajar with his boot. His broad shoulders seemed to fill the door frame, and she immediately released the handle as if she'd touched a hot stove.

"Excuse us," Sawyer Plank apologized in a softer tone. He stepped aside, revealing three towheaded children who each looked to be about seven years old. "Sarah, Samuel and Simon are to begin school today."

He watched the fear melt from the woman's expression as she surveyed the triplets. "*Wilkom.* I'm Hannah Lantz," she said, as much to them as to him.

"Guder mariye," the three children chorused.

"I'm Sawyer Plank," he explained. "Nephew of John Plank."

"Of course." She nodded, tipping her chin upward to look at him. He couldn't help but notice something sorrowful about her intensely blue eyes, despite her cheerful tone. "We've been expecting you."

"I apologize for being late," Sawyer said. Then, so quietly as to be a whisper, he confided, "I had to fix Sarah's hair myself, and it took longer than I expected."

Hannah narrowed her eyes quizzically.

"I'm afraid my hands are better suited for making cabinets than for arranging a young girl's hair." He held out his rough, square hands, palms up, as if to present proof.

Hannah's eyes darted from them to Sarah's crooked part. "You've done well," she commented graciously, although he noticed she was biting her lip. "Sarah, please take a seat next to Abigail Stolzfus, at the front of the class. Samuel and Simon, you may sit at the empty desks near the window."

Sawyer thrust a small paper bag that was straining at the seams in Hannah's direction. "It's their lunch," he explained, still speaking in a low tone so as not to be heard by the children.

"My *onkel* made it because, as you may know, my *ant* is deceased, so I'm not sure what the lunch consists of. Ordinarily my youngest sister, Gertrude, takes care of such things in Ohio. She would have accompanied us here, too, but shortly before my *onkel* broke his leg, it was nearing time for my eldest sister, Kathryn, to deliver her *bobbel*, so Gertrude traveled to Indiana to keep her household running smoothly."

Although he was usually a private man of few words, Sawyer couldn't seem to stop himself from rambling to the petite, dark-haired teacher whose eyes were so blue they nearly matched the shade of violet dress she wore beneath her apron.

"I'm not much of a farmer, but as soon as I heard John needed help, I put my foreman in charge of the shop," he continued, neglecting to add that the timing couldn't have been worse, since he had just lost one of his carpenters to an *Englisch* competitor who constantly threatened to put Sawyer out of business. "The *kinner* and I immediately set out for Pennsylvania. We only arrived on Saturday evening."

He was quiet as he wiped the sweat from his brow with his sleeve.

"It was *gut* of you to come help your *onkel* during harvest season," Hannah commented. "If there's nothing else, I will see to it the *kinner* divide the lunch evenly between them."

Sawyer sensed he was being dismissed, and he was only too relieved for the opportunity to end the conversation. "I won't be late picking them up," he muttered as he turned to leave.

Once he was in his buggy, he flicked the reins with one hand and simultaneously slapped his knee in disgust with the other. What was wrong with him, babbling on about Sarah's hair and his work as a cabinetmaker? No doubt Hannah Lantz thought he was vain as well as tardy.

He hadn't meant to sound boastful about dropping everything in Blue Hill in order to help his uncle, either. John was family and family helped each other, no matter what. Just like when John came to Ohio and kept the shop running smoothly after Sawyer's mother and father died six years earlier, and again when he lost his beloved wife, Eliza, three years later. It was an honor—not a burden—to assist his uncle now. He only wished Gertrude hadn't gone to Indiana, so the children could have stayed in Ohio with her. Sarah had had nightmares ever since Gertrude left, and the boys had grown so thin without her cooking.

But he knew there was no sense focusing on the way he wished things were. In all these years, no amount of regret had ever brought his Eliza back. He trusted God's timing and plans were always perfect, even if they were sometimes painful to endure. His duty was to accept the circumstances set before him.

But that didn't mean he couldn't try to make a difficult situation better. As the horse clopped down the lane to his uncle's farm, Sawyer devised a plan so he could spend as many hours as possible in the fields. If the weather and crops cooperated, he'd help finish harvesting in six weeks instead of eight or more, so his family could return to Ohio at the first opportunity.

As the children barreled outside for lunch hour, the paper bag Simon was carrying split down the middle, spilling the Planks' unwrapped cheese and meat sandwiches onto the ground, so Hannah invited the children to join her for sweet bread inside the classroom. She marveled at how quickly they devoured the bread and preserves.

"Do you have such appetites in Ohio?" she inquired, aware the children seemed thinner than most.

"*Ant* Gertrude doesn't bake bread like this," Samuel said, his cheeks full. "She says it's because her *mamm* died before she could learn her the best way to make it."

"Before she could *teach* her," Sarah corrected.

"Our *mamm* died, too," offered Simon seriously. "She's with the Lord."

"As is my *mamm*," Hannah murmured.

"Did your *mamm* teach you how to make bread before she died?" asked Samuel.

"*Neh*, but my *groossmammi* did. See? *Gott* always provides."

"I wish I had a *groossmammi* to teach me." Sarah sighed. "*Daed* said *Groossmammi* died when we were as little as chicks that didn't even have their feathers yet."

"I'm happy to share my bread with you," Hannah told Sarah. "Eating it is better than baking it anyway. Now that you're done, why don't you go outside and play with the other *kinner*."

Doris passed them as they exited. "What darling little things," she remarked to Hannah. "They must be triplets."

"*Jah*. Their names are Samuel, Sarah and Simon Plank," Hannah replied.

"So you've met the wealthy widower?"

"He has a name, too. It's Sawyer. We spoke briefly this morning."

"What did you think of him?" wheedled Doris. "Give me your honest opinion."

"Well, I didn't have my tape measure with me, so I can't confirm whether he's over six feet tall," Hannah answered evasively, although she knew exactly what Doris was getting at.

"*Schnickelfritz!*" Doris taunted. "I meant, what did you think of him as a potential suitor?"

"I *didn't* think of him as a potential suitor," Hannah emphasized. "I thought of him as the *daed* of my scholars, a nephew of John Plank and a guest in our district."

"He's not to your liking, then?" Doris persisted.

"I didn't say that!" Hannah was too exasperated to elaborate.

Fortunately, she didn't have to, as Eli opened the door at that moment, yawping, "Caleb got hit with a ball and it knocked his tooth out."

Doris covered her mouth with the back of her hand. "You'll have to handle it," she directed Hannah. "You know that kind of thing makes me woozy."

"Of course," Hannah calmly agreed. "But you'll need to get used to it soon, since *kinner* lose their baby teeth all the time. It's all part of caring for 'darling little things' at that age."

After they'd eaten lunch, John urged Sawyer to join him on the porch before returning to the fields.

"It's never too hot or too late for coffee," he said, hobbling toward him with a crutch under one arm and a mug sloshing precariously in his other hand.

Sawyer accepted the strong, hot drink. Brewing coffee appeared to be his uncle's only culinary skill; from what Sawyer had tasted so far, the food he prepared was marginally palatable, although there was certainly a lot of it.

"I've been thinking," Sawyer started. "I'd like to hire a young woman to watch the *kinner* after school. She can transport them home in the afternoon and cook our supper, as well."

"Our meals don't suit you?" joshed John.

"*Jah*, the food is ample and hearty," he answered quickly, not wanting to insult his host. He launched into an earnest explanation. "But since you can't get into and out of the buggy without an adult to assist you, it would be easier to have someone else pick them up from school in the afternoon. This way, my work will only be interrupted in the morning, not in the morning and afternoon both. If the woman I hire is going to care for the *kinner* in the afternoon, she may as well fix us supper, too."

John chortled. "Trust me, Sawyer, I understand. The boys and I haven't had a decent meal since my Lydia died five years ago. But they're teenagers and they'll eat anything. How did you get on without Gertrude these last few weeks in Ohio?"

"I hired their friend's *mamm* to mind the *kinner* with her own while I was in the shop during the day, but evenings were chaotic," Sawyer admitted. "You can guess what the cooking was like by how scrawny the *kinner* are."

"You need a full-time wife, not a part-time cook," John ribbed him. "Someone who will keep you company, not just keep your house."

"So I've been told," Sawyer replied noncommittally. His uncle was only a few years older than he was, and they good-naturedly badgered each other like brothers. "I imagine you've been given the same advice yourself?"

"*Jah*, but I live in withering Willow Creek, not in thriving Blue Hill. Isn't there a matchmaker who can pair you with one of the many unmarried women in your town?"

Chuckling self-consciously, Sawyer confessed, "After a dozen attempts, the matchmaker declared me a useless cause, much to Gertrude's dismay."

He'd found his lifetime match when he'd met Eliza, the love of his life and mother of his children. But rather than try to explain, he offered John the excuse he'd made so frequently he half believed it himself. "I can't be distracted by a woman. I have a cabinetry shop to run, employees to oversee. Their livelihood depends on me, and business is tough. But Gertrude is at that age where her mind is filled with romantic notions about love and courting, probably more for herself than for me."

"My sons are at that age, too," John said. "It's only natural."

"Perhaps," Sawyer agreed. But he wanted to protect his sister from the risk that came with loving someone so much that losing the person caused unimaginable grief. She was too young to experience that kind of pain.

Besides, as long as Gertrude lived with them, he didn't have to worry about the children being raised without a female presence in the house. His sister tended to their every need, as much like their older sibling as their aunt.

Aloud he said, "I'll arrange to hire someone as soon as possible. Do you have any recommendations?"

"Most of the women in Willow Creek are married with *kinner* and farms of their own, and they live too far from here to make transporting your *kinner* worth anyone's while. Either that, or the younger *meed* need to watch their siblings," John replied. "But Hannah Lantz, the schoolteacher, lives nearby and she's unmarried. She's very capable to boot."

Sawyer suppressed the urge to balk. There was something about the winsome teacher that unsettled him, although perhaps it was only that he hadn't gotten off on the right foot with her by showing up late to school.

"Are you sure she's the only one?"

"Not unless you want Doris Hooley fawning over you."

"Who's she?"

"She's the upper-grade schoolteacher. You haven't met her yet?"

"Neh," Sawyer answered. "Not yet."

"Consider yourself fortunate." John grinned. "I don't know her well, but it's rumored she can be very…attentive. Especially toward unmarried men."

A woman's amorous attention was the last thing Sawyer

wanted. Deciding he'd present his employment proposition to Hannah that afternoon, he downed the last of his drink.

"If only I were half as strong as your coffee," he joked, "the fields would be harvested in no time."

But the work was so grueling that Sawyer lost track of time and returned to the schoolhouse nearly an hour after the rest of the students had departed. The boys were tossing a ball between them and Sarah was sitting on the steps, her head nestled against Hannah's arm as Hannah read a book aloud to her.

When he hopped down from his buggy and started across the lawn, Hannah rose and the children raced in his direction.

"I told Sarah not to worry—there was a *gut* reason you were late," Hannah said.

Her statement sounded more like a question, and whatever vulnerable quality he noticed in her face earlier was replaced by a different emotion. Anger, perhaps? Or was it merely annoyance? Whatever it was, Sawyer once again felt disarmed by the look in her eyes—which were rimmed with long, thick lashes—as if she could see right through him.

"Forgive my tardiness," he apologized, without offering an explanation. He didn't have a valid excuse, nor did he want to start rambling again. He needed to make a good impression if he wanted her to consider becoming a nanny to his children.

"I notice there's another buggy in the yard," he observed. "Is it yours?"

"It's Doris Hooley's," she responded curtly. "She's the upper-grade teacher."

"In that case, may I offer you a ride home?"

"*Denki*, but *neh*. I have tasks to finish inside. Besides, it seems as if your horse trots slower than I can walk,"

Hannah answered in a tone that was neither playful nor entirely serious. "Samuel, Simon and Sarah, I will see you in the morning, *Gott* willing."

She turned on her heel, gathered her skirt and scurried back up the steps into the schoolhouse. Inside the classroom, she quickly gathered a sheaf of papers and stuffed them into her satchel.

She knew she hadn't acted very charitably, but Sawyer Plank seemed an unreliable man, turning up late, twice in one day, without so much as an explanation or excuse for his second offense. Did he think because he was a wealthy business owner, common courtesies didn't apply to him? Or perhaps in Ohio, folks didn't honor their word, but in Willow Creek, people did what they said they were going to do. Not to mention, Sarah was fretting miserably that something terrible had happened to detain her father. It was very inconsiderate of him to keep them all waiting like that.

As Hannah picked up an eraser to clean the chalkboard, Doris sashayed into the room. Although she lived in the opposite direction, she had volunteered to bring Hannah home. Hannah suspected Doris wanted an excuse to dilly-dally until Sawyer arrived so she could size him up. But whatever the reason behind Doris's gesture, Hannah was grateful for the transportation home on such a muggy afternoon.

"Where have the triplets gone?" Doris inquired. "I thought they were with you."

"They just left with their *daed*."

"Ach! I must have been in the washroom when he came to retrieve them," Doris whined.

They were interrupted by a hesitant rapping at the door—Sawyer hadn't left after all. He removed his hat and waited to be invited in. Hannah hoped he hadn't heard their discussion.

"You may enter. I won't bite." Doris tee-heed. "I'm Doris Hooley."

She was so tall her eyes were nearly even with Sawyer's, and Hannah couldn't help but notice she batted her lashes repeatedly.

"Guder nammidaag," he replied courteously.

She tittered. "You remind me of a little boy on his first day of school, so nervous you forget to tell the class your name."

Apparently unfazed by Doris's brash remark, Sawyer straightened his shoulders and responded, "I am Sawyer Plank, nephew of John Plank, and I'm sorry to interrupt, but I need to ask Hannah something concerning the *kinner*."

"Of course," Hannah agreed. Although she had no idea what he wanted to request of her, she felt strangely smug that Sawyer had sought her out in front of Doris. "What is it?"

"As you may have guessed, my work on the farm makes it inconvenient for me to pick up the *kinner* after school," he began. He continued to explain he considered delivering the children to school to be a necessary interruption of his morning farmwork, but that he hoped to hire someone to transport them home and oversee them after school through the evening meal.

"She also would be expected to prepare a meal for all of us, but I would pay more than a fair wage. Of course, she would be invited to eat with us, as well."

He hardly had spoken his last word when Doris suggested, "I'd be pleased to provide the *kinner's* care. I have daily use of a buggy and horse and could readily bring them to the farm when school is over for the day. I think you'll find I'm a fine cook, too."

Sawyer opened his mouth and closed it twice before stammering, "I'm sorry, but you've misunderstood. I—I—"

"I believe he was offering the opportunity to me, since I'm the *kinner's* teacher and they'll be more familiar with me," Hannah broke in. Despite her initial misgivings about Sawyer, she was absolutely certain this was the provision she'd been praying to receive. She didn't give the matter a second thought before adding, "And I agree to do it."

"I see," Doris retorted in a frosty tone directed at Hannah. "Well, I'll leave the two of you alone to discuss your arrangement further."

"*Denki.* I will stop by your classroom as soon as I'm ready to leave," Hannah confirmed.

Before exiting, Doris turned to Sawyer and brazenly hinted, "With Hannah watching the triplets, I hope you find you have time for socializing with your neighbors here in Willow Creek."

No sooner had Doris flounced away than Hannah confessed, "I was being hasty. I shouldn't have accepted your offer. I'm terribly sorry, but I can't possibly help you."

"Why not? If it's a matter of salary, I assure you I'll pay you plentifully and—"

"*Neh*, it isn't that," Hannah insisted. "It's…my *grooss-daadi*. I have a responsibility to him. I must keep our house, make our supper… He is old and deaf. He can't manage on his own. And unlike Doris, I don't have daily transportation. Our buggy is showing signs of wear and the horse is getting old, so we limit taking them out for essential trips only."

Sawyer was quiet a moment, his eyes scanning her face. She looked as downcast as he felt.

"Suppose the *kinner* come home from school with you

and stay until after supper? Would your *groossdaadi* object? I would collect them each evening. They could help you with your household chores and they wouldn't make any—"

"Jah!" she interrupted, beaming. "I will have to ask *Groossdaadi*, but I don't think he'll object. I'll need a few days to confirm it with him and make preparations. Perhaps I could begin next Monday?"

"Absolutely." Sawyer grinned. "Now, would you please permit the *kinner* and me to give you a ride home? I'll need to know where you live in order to pick them up on Monday."

She hesitated before saying, "*Denki*, but Doris has already offered."

"Are you certain?" he persisted.

Just then, a flash of lightning brightened the room and Hannah dropped the eraser she was holding, effectively halting their conversation. "I'm certain," she stated. "You mustn't keep your *kinner* waiting any longer. They've been so patient already."

Sawyer was taken aback by the sudden shift in Hannah's demeanor. As he darted through the spitting rain, he thought that her countenance was like the weather itself; one minute her expression was sunny and clear, but the next it was clouded and dark. He wasn't quite sure what to make of her at all, but at least his worries about the children's care had subsided for the time being.

Chapter Two

Because Doris gave her a ride home from school, Hannah arrived early enough to prepare one of her grandfather's favorite meals: ground beef and cabbage skillet and apple dumplings. Making supper kept her distracted from the peals of thunder that sounded in the distance, and so did thinking about Sawyer and the children.

She supposed she could have accepted his offer to bring her home, instead of imposing on Doris. But what kind of example would she have been to the children—a grown woman, afraid of a storm? Hadn't she reminded Sarah several times that day to trust in the Lord when she was worried about her father? Yet there Hannah was, trembling like a leaf because of a little thunder.

She realized there was a second reason she hesitated to ride with Sawyer: she worried what kind of foolish thing she might say. She didn't know what had caused her to joke about his horse's speed, but she couldn't risk offending him, especially as he might be her new employer. Thinking about the slight smile that lit his serious, handsome face made her stomach flutter. She retrieved her satchel from its hook in search of a piece of bread, but then remembered she'd given her last crust to Simon, who gobbled it up in four bites.

When her grandfather entered the kitchen, his first

words were not unlike those she had cast at Sawyer, but his tone was much gruffer.

"What is your reason for being so late?" he barked.

Because her grandfather had lost his hearing years ago, he had no sense of the volume of his voice—at least, that was what Hannah chose to believe.

"I'm sorry, *Groossdaadi.* I was helping my new scholars." She looked at him directly when she spoke. Although her grandfather was adept at reading lips, she knew from experience a brief answer was the best reply, especially when he seemed agitated.

"Is dinner going to be late again?" he complained, despite the early hour.

Please, Lord, give him patience. And me, too, she prayed.

"*Neh.* It is almost done."

"Gut," he grunted. "You left me here with hardly a morsel of bread."

Hannah knew the claim was preposterous; she fixed him a sizable lunch before leaving for school, and there was always freshly made bread in the bread box. Thinking about it made her remember Sarah's desire to learn how to bake bread. Hannah hadn't been exactly accurate when she'd said it was more fun to eat than to bake. Eating freshly baked bread was a pleasure, but smelling it baking was equally appealing.

She realized because her grandfather was deaf, he probably looked forward to having his other senses stimulated. Adding a little extra garlic to the skillet to enhance the aroma, she began to sing, and by the time she and her grandfather were seated, the storm had blown over.

After saying grace, she touched her grandfather's arm to get his attention. He dug into his meal, chewing as he watched her lips.

"*Gott* has provided us help with our income," she said, knowing that if she prefaced her proposal by indicating it was from the Lord, her grandfather would be less inclined to say no. "I have been asked to watch the *kinner* of Sawyer Plank. He is John Plank's nephew, the one who is helping him harvest until his leg heals."

Her grandfather shoveled a few forkfuls of meat into his mouth. When he looked up again, Hannah continued.

"I will need to bring them home with me after school—"

"Neh," her grandfather refused, lifting his glass of milk. Unlike most Amish, they had always been too poor to afford their own milk cow, but for generations the Zook family had made it a faithful practice to deliver a fresh bottle—often with a chunk of cheese—to their milk bin.

As her grandfather took a big swallow, Hannah finished speaking, undaunted. "They will stay here through supper time. Then Sawyer will pick them up."

"Neh," her grandfather repeated. "I will not have *kinner* in my house."

Hannah curled her fingers into a fist beneath the table, digging her fingernails into her palm. She knew how much her grandfather disliked having children around—after all, he'd reminded her and her younger sister, Eve, of that fact repeatedly when they were growing up. She waited until he'd had a second helping of beef and cabbage, and then she dished him up the biggest, gooiest apple dumpling before she attempted to persuade him again.

"Groossdaadi," she pleaded, her eyes expressing the urgency he couldn't hear in her voice. "I promise to keep them outside as much as possible. They will help with the chores. The boys will stack wood and clean the coop and do whatever else you need them to do. I will see to it they don't disturb you in your workshop."

This time her grandfather merely shook his head as he

cut into the tender dumpling with the side of his fork. The crust oozed with sweet fruit.

"I know how hard you've worked to provide for us," Hannah said, tugging on his sleeve to make him read her lips. "But I've stretched our budget as far as I can, and it will only get worse when I am no longer a teacher. Please, *Groossdaadi*, let me do my part and earn this income."

As he ate the rest of his dessert, Hannah sent up a silent prayer. *Please, Lord, let him agree to what I've asked.* When he pushed his chair back across the floor, the scraping sound sent a chill up her spine, but she remained hopeful.

"They'd better not make too much noise," he warned crossly before retiring for the evening.

Hannah had to bite her tongue to keep from retorting, "But, *Groossdaadi*, how would you know if they did?" Having grown up under his thumb, she understood what he'd meant: he wouldn't permit them to make nuisances of themselves.

She threw her arms around his neck and looked him in the eye. "I will see to it they don't," she promised.

"Bah," he muttered, but he didn't pull away from her embrace until she let him go.

On the way home, when Sawyer asked the children how their first day at school was, they all spoke at once.

"We made friends with some other boys," Samuel said.

"Eli and Caleb. They said they have a German shepherd, and it had six puppies," Simon announced. "Can we have a puppy, *Daed*?"

"It's '*may* we.' Teacher says we're supposed to say '*may* I,' not '*can* I.' A *can* is something you store food in," Sarah corrected him. "I made a new friend, too, *Daed*. Her name is Abigail, but she said I can call her—I *may* call her—Abby."

Distracting the children from their request for a puppy—Gertrude was allergic—Sawyer commented, "It sounds as if you've already learned something from your teacher, too?"

"Jah," Samuel agreed. "We learned how to bat a ball after lunch hour! The teacher can hit it farther than anyone else, even the boys from the upper classes!"

"And she fixed my hair, see?" Sarah twisted in her seat to show him where her hair was neatly tucked into a bun. "It didn't hurt a bit, even the snarled parts. The teacher said her *mamm* taught her how to brush them out when she was a girl my age. Her hair is dark like a crow's and wavy, but mine is light like hay and straight, but she said her secret brushing method works on all colors of hair and all sizes of tangles."

As minor of a matter as grooming was, even Gertrude complained about how much Sarah always wiggled when she was combing her hair. During Gertrude's absence, Sawyer often had to refrain from using a harsh tone to make Sarah sit still. The small but important empathy Hannah demonstrated to his daughter by carefully fixing her bun seemed like a promising indicator of the care she'd provide as their nanny.

After they arrived home, the children helped with chores around the farm: Sarah swept the floors and sorted and washed vegetables, and the boys cleaned the chicken coop, stacked firewood and helped in the stable. Their chores in Ohio were similar, but because they lived on a modest plot of land in a neighborhood instead of in a large farmhouse on sizable acreage, their new assignments in Pennsylvania took them much longer to complete. Simon and Samuel usually had boundless energy, but by supper time, they were too weary to lift their chins from their chests at the table.

"Try a second helping of beef stew," Sawyer urged them.

"I'm too tired to chew," Samuel protested.

Simon asked, "May we go to bed?"

"Look," Sawyer pointed out. "*Onkel* bought special apple fry pies from Yoder's Bakery in town. You may have one if you eat a little more meat."

"*Denki, Onkel.* That was very thoughtful of you," Sarah said, imitating a phrase Sawyer knew she'd learned from Gertrude. "But I couldn't eat another bite."

"No promises the pies will be here tomorrow," Sawyer's cousin Phillip warned.

"We survived for five years without our *mamm* here to cook for us," Jonas, Sawyer's other cousin, scoffed. "You shouldn't coddle them, Sawyer, particularly the boys."

Sawyer got the feeling Jonas resented the children's presence, but he couldn't fault Simon, Samuel and Sarah for being too tired to eat; he, too, was exhausted from the day's events.

Still, he didn't believe in wasting food, and when Simon chased a chunk of beef around his bowl with his spoon, Sawyer directed, "Sit up and eat your meal. *Waste not, want not*, as your *mamm* always said."

"I'm not hungry." The boy sighed.

Sawyer warned, "You need to eat so you can do well in school tomorrow."

"He'll just ask the teacher for a piece of sweet bread instead," Sarah said. "Like she gave him today."

"Sarah, it's not kind to tattle," Samuel reminded her. "Besides, the teacher gave us *all* a piece of bread."

"*Jah*, but she gave Simon an extra piece in the afternoon," Sarah reported. "The very last piece, smothered in strawberry preserves. Teacher says strawberries taste like pink sunshine."

"Sweets in the afternoon before supper," Jonas scoffed. "No wonder they turn up their noses at meat and potatoes. Pass me his serving. My appetite hasn't been spoiled and neither have I."

Simon ducked his head as he handed over his bowl. He had a small freckle on the top of his left earlobe, whereas Samuel had none. It was how Sawyer could tell the two boys apart when they were infants. Watching Simon's ears purpling with shame, Sawyer felt a small qualm about Hannah. Well-intentioned as the gesture may have been, Sawyer wondered if it represented her common practice. He couldn't allow her to continue to ply the children with sweets instead of wholesome meals if he expected them to grow healthier under her care, and he decided to speak to her about it when he saw her next.

After supper, Hannah's grandfather retired to his room to read Scripture as she washed the dishes and swept the floors. She folded the linens she had hung out to dry that morning before leaving for school. As she was putting them away, she passed the room that used to be Eve's. Spread on the bed was one of the quilts her younger sister had made. Although it was darker and plainer than those she fashioned to sell to tourists, there was no mistaking her meticulous stitching and patterns.

Hannah had never developed the superior sewing abilities Eve possessed. As the eldest, she was tasked with putting supper on the table, gardening, caring for Eve and meeting her grandfather's needs. Not that she minded; she felt indebted to her grandfather for raising her and Eve, and she knew the Lord provided everyone with different talents. She admired her sister's handiwork a moment longer before closing the bedroom door with a sigh. How Hannah missed Eve's chatter ever since she moved to Lancaster to set up house with her husband last year.

But at least now that Hannah would be watching the Plank children and she had lessons to plan and students' work to review, the evenings wouldn't seem to last forever, as they did during the summer months.

Kneeling by her bed, she prayed, Denki, *Lord, for Your providing for* Groossdaadi *and me, as You have always done. Please help me to be a* gut *nanny to Sarah, Simon and Samuel.*

She removed her prayer *kapp* and hung it on her headboard before sliding between the sheets. A loud rumble of thunder caused her nightstand to vibrate, and she closed her eyes before lightning illuminated the room. No matter how hard she tried to push the memory from her mind, the metallic smell in the air always brought her back to the night her mother and father perished when lightning struck the tree under which they'd sought shelter during a rainstorm. She had been such a young girl when it happened that the memory of the storm itself was more vivid than almost any recollection she had of her parents prior to their deaths.

She rolled onto her side and buried her face in the pillow, much like Sarah had buried her face in Hannah's sleeve when Sawyer failed to show up on time. Hannah wondered if Sarah was insecure because Sawyer was an unreliable parent or merely because she was anxious about being a newcomer. The boys seemed to be more outgoing than their sister was. They adjusted to their lessons magnificently and joined the games during lunch hour. But Sarah seemed uncertain, trying to say and do everything perfectly and in constant need of reassurance from Hannah. She supposed the girl might have been feeling at a loss without any other females on the farm, and she decided to do her best to serve as a role model for her.

Raindrops riveted the windowpane, and although the air was sultry, Hannah pulled the quilt over her head, mussing her hair. She recalled how Sarah's bun had come undone during lunch hour. Hannah giggled, imagining Sawyer struggling to pin his daughter's hair in place. Then, as she thought of his large, masculine hands, a shiver tickled her spine. The suddenness of it surprised her, but she attributed it to the change in air temperature.

Before drifting off, she anticipated showing the children the shortcut home from school and studying insects and birds along the way. She imagined teaching Sarah how to make sweet bread and chasing squirrels with Samuel and Simon. They would grow sturdy from her meals and smart from her tutelage. She would sing hymns and read stories to them on rainy afternoons. It would be like teaching, only different: it would be, she supposed, more like being a mother than she'd ever been. Now that she actually had the opportunity, she had to admit, she could hardly wait!

Sawyer felt as if a huge burden had been lifted from his shoulders. As he knelt beside his bed, he prayed, *Thank You, Lord, for Hannah's willingness to care for the* kinner. *Please work in her* groossdaadi's *heart to agree to it, as well. Bless Kathryn and her family, especially the baby, and keep watch over Gertrude. Please keep the crew safe and productive in Ohio.*

Praying about his employees, Sawyer exhaled loudly. Upon returning to the farm that afternoon, he had discovered a soggy express-mail letter in the box from his foreman reporting that one of his crew members severed his finger the day Sawyer left for Pennsylvania. *Due to being short staffed already, we are falling even further behind on orders*, the note said. It was another urgent reminder to Sawyer that he needed to hasten his work with his cousins so he could return home as soon as possible. At least being able to work longer days without interruptions would help with that.

He was relieved that Hannah, in particular, possibly would be watching the children. He owed her a debt of gratitude for rescuing him from Doris's clutches. He had known women like Doris in Ohio, who seemed to use the children's welfare as an excuse to call on him and Gertrude. At least, that was what Gertrude had claimed on a few occasions.

"I thought you wanted me to marry again," he teased one afternoon after Gertrude was irked by a female visitor who stopped by with a heaping tray of oatmeal whoopee pie cookies *and* an entire "sawdust pie." (When the woman found out Sawyer wasn't present, she took the sweets home without allowing the children or Gertrude to sample so much as a bite.)

"I *do* want you to marry again," Gertrude insisted. "But I want you to marry someone genuine, like Eliza."

There will never be anyone as genuine as Eliza, he thought.

Take Hannah, for instance. Whereas Eliza was soft-spoken and reserved, Hannah seemed a bit cheeky, which made it difficult to discern how sincere she was. Sawyer supposed Hannah was used to teasing men for sport; someone as becoming as she was no doubt found favor with the opposite gender, especially because she appeared competent and helpful, as well. Yet, surprisingly, she was unmarried—Sawyer ruefully imagined her suitors probably were tardy arriving to court her, so she turned them away.

Lightning reflected off the white sheets on Sawyer's

bed and thunder shook the walls. He stretched his neck, listening for Sarah's cries, but there were none. He figured she was too exhausted to stir.

Sawyer's thoughts drifted to the dark tendrils framing Hannah's face that afternoon. They had probably come loose when she was playing ball with her students. He supposed someone who earned the affection of his daughter and the admiration of his sons in one day deserved his high regard, too. It wasn't her fault she was so pretty; he recognized he shouldn't judge her for that.

He remembered how Hannah suddenly hurried him out the door that afternoon. Despite her authority in the classroom and her outspoken joshing, there was something unmistakably vulnerable in her eyes. But he had no doubt she'd take excellent care of Simon, Samuel and Sarah—especially once he restricted the amount of treats she served them—for the short time they were visiting Pennsylvania.

As the sky released its torrents, Sawyer's contented sigh turned into a yawn and he rolled onto his side. He slumbered through the night, waking only once when he had a dream of bread smothered in strawberry jam that was so real, he almost thought he could taste its sweetness on his lips.

The next morning, Hannah rose early to prepare a hearty breakfast for her grandfather, and she set aside an ample lunch, too. If Sawyer Plank was tardy again after school, she didn't want her grandfather to accuse her of neglecting his appetite. She ate only a small portion herself in order to stretch their food budget, but she took the bread crusts with her. At lunch, she'd spread them with the preserves Abigail had given her, an indulgent treat these days.

She scuttled the mile and a half to the school yard from

her home. Built on the corner of the Zook farm, the tiny house and plot of land were all her grandfather had ever been able to afford. But Jeremiah Zook had always granted Hannah and Eve access to the rolling meadow, thriving stream and dense copse of trees on the south side of the property. The setting provided the young sisters a serene and spacious haven from their grandfather's unrelenting demands.

As an adult, Hannah still chose to zigzag across the acreage on her way to and from school instead of taking the main roads. She always felt she could breathe deeper and think more clearly after strolling the grassy and wooded paths she knew by heart.

The weather was still unseasonably warm, and her upper lip beaded with perspiration as she picked her way across the final damp field. From a distance, she could see a single buggy in the lane by the school, which was strange since Doris was usually the last to arrive and the first to leave. As she drew nearer, she spotted three familiar blond heads, bobbing in and out from behind the trees during a game of tag. Sawyer was perched on the steps.

"Guder mariye," she greeted him, before adding, "Your horse's legs must have healed. You're early."

A peculiar look passed across Sawyer's face, and Hannah immediately regretted her comment. She had meant it to be playful, not vexing. There was something so solemn about his demeanor she couldn't help but try to elicit a little levity.

"If we're too early, I will wait with the *kinner* until you're ready for them to come inside," he replied seriously.

"*Neh*, you mustn't do that," she said by way of apology, but then recognized it seemed as if she were dismissing him from the yard. She quickly explained, "You are free to leave the *kinner* or to stay with them as long as you wish.

You're free to stay with them outside, that is—not in the classroom. Unless you also need help with your spelling or mathematics."

There she went again! Insulting him when she only meant to break the ice. This time, however, a smile played at the corner of his lips.

"My spelling and mathematics are strong," he said. "It's only my time-telling that suffers."

"Your time-telling is already improving," Hannah said generously. "I notice you're working on your daughter's grooming skills, as well. I don't mean to intrude on your efforts, but if Sarah's hair should need additional straightening, would you allow me to complete the task?"

"Allow you? I would *wilkom* you," he insisted. "It's no intrusion. Especially if you are to become the *kinner's* nanny."

His enthusiasm delighted Hannah, who tipped her head upward to meet his eyes. "I'm glad you mentioned that," she trilled. "Because my *groossdaadi* has agreed that I may watch the *kinner* after school, beginning Monday."

"That's *wunderbaar*!" Sawyer boomed, and again Hannah was warmed by his unbridled earnestness.

Just then, Simon skidded to a stop in between them and thrust his fist up toward his father.

"Look! Have you ever seen such a big toad?"

"It *is* huge," Hannah acknowledged, studying the boy's catch. "It's the same color as the dirt. You must have keen eyesight to be able to spot him."

The little boy modestly replied, "I didn't know he was there at first, but then I saw something hopping and that's when I grabbed him."

Samuel and Sarah circled Simon to get another look.

"Not too tight, Simon. You're squeezing him," Sawyer cautioned. "You must be careful not to harm it."

As he spoke, Hannah felt his warm breath on the nape of her neck as she bent over the amphibian. She hadn't realized Sawyer was standing in such close proximity, and she was overcome with a peculiar sensation of dizziness.

She stepped backward and announced, "You ought to release him now, Simon. Be sure to wipe your hands, please."

With that, she darted up the steps and into the classroom. *"Mach's gut,"* she said, bidding Sawyer goodbye over her shoulder.

As the horse made its way back to the farm, Sawyer rubbed his forehead. Hannah had ended the conversation so abruptly he didn't have a chance to speak to her about not giving the children treats. He had no idea what caused her brusque departure, although he noticed she visibly recoiled when he scolded Simon; had she thought him too strict?

Eliza at times had grimaced when he'd corrected the children as youngsters. They had spoken about it once toward the end of her illness, after the triplets were asleep and Eliza herself was lying in bed.

"Of course, *kinner* must be disciplined to obey their parents," she said when he asked for her opinion. "It is our greatest responsibility to train them in what is right and to keep them safe."

"But?" he questioned.

"But, my dear Sawyer." Eliza sighed. "You are so tall and the *kinner* so small—sometimes it seems you don't realize the strength of your own voice. I know how gentle you are, but to *kinner* or to strangers, a single loud word may be perceived as threatening as the growl of a bear."

She had been right: Sawyer admitted he hadn't realized the intimidating effect of his size and volume. He'd raised his hands like two giant paws and let out a roar to make Eliza laugh, which she did, as weak as she was. After that, he made a concentrated effort to speak in a low but firm voice, but perhaps this morning his volume had been too loud?

Then he asked himself why he should be bothered about what Hannah Lantz thought of him. She was a virtual stranger. Besides, *Gott* knew the intention of his heart, just as Eliza had always known.

Troubled he'd found himself comparing Eliza and Hannah, Sawyer was glad for the heavy field work that lay before him, which allowed him to pour all of his energy into the physical labor and sufficiently rid his mind of memories of Eliza and notions about Hannah.

By late afternoon, the air was oppressive with humidity, and as Sawyer rode toward the schoolhouse, a line of clouds billowed across the horizon. He was neither early nor late for dismissal; as he approached, several children scampered across the yard and climbed into buggies parked beneath the willow. After waiting a few minutes without seeing Sarah, Samuel and Simon, he jumped down and strode toward the building. A few hot raindrops splashed against his skin before he tentatively pushed the door open.

Inside, the children were paying rapt attention as Hannah read aloud to them from a book opened in her lap. He had never seen the boys sit so still. When Sawyer cleared his throat, she glanced up in his direction, her eyes dancing.

"Here is your *daed* now, Sarah," she said. "Didn't I tell you he'd arrive on time?"

"I was waiting outside," he explained, removing his hat. "You told me earlier I wasn't to come indoors."

She tilted her head and pursed her lips in the curious manner she had a way of doing, and then recognition swept over her expression. "Not during lessons, *neh*, but you are allowed—indeed, you are *wilkom*—to come in after school. It's no intrusion."

Her repetition of the same phrases he'd used earlier that morning gave him pause. Did he dare to think she was deliberately being facetious? If so, it was difficult to tell; her quips were far subtler and more amusing than Doris's overt coquetry.

His mouth was so dry, all he could muster was *"Denki,"* and this time he was the one who departed abruptly without saying another word.

Chapter Three

The warm weather caused the yeast to rise quickly. As Hannah kneaded the dough the following morning, she racked her mind for recipes she could make once Simon, Samuel and Sarah arrived. She had been so thrilled that she'd convinced her grandfather to allow her to watch the Plank children that she'd neglected the practical details involved in the arrangement. Every month, she budgeted their meal allowance down to the penny; she didn't know where the money would come from to feed her grandfather and herself as well as the children. As it was, she wouldn't receive the next installment of her teacher's salary until the first of October.

"I should bring your toys to the shop on Saturday," Hannah mouthed to her grandfather when he looked up from his plate of eggs and potatoes at breakfast.

It wasn't too early for tourists to begin shopping for Christmas during their excursions through the countryside. The sooner Hannah's grandfather put the wooden trains, tractors and dollhouses on consignment, the better. She also hoped one of the toys her *groossdaadi* put on consignment last month sold, which would help supplement the cost of groceries for the upcoming week.

"I'll take you," he shouted, wiping his face with a napkin.

She had hoped to go alone; his handling of the buggy

made her nervous. He couldn't hear passing traffic and many a car had to swerve to avoid hitting him when he should have yielded. Also, he bellowed so loudly to the shopkeeper, the poor man cringed and shrugged, which frustrated her grandfather. Hannah inevitably had to translate.

"Are you certain? I expect it will be a very hot and busy day."

"Am I certain?" he repeated. "I am certain of this—my toys put food on the table. If I am to get the best price, I must accompany you. Unless you wish us to starve as I nearly did yesterday?"

Even if her grandfather had been able to hear, she wouldn't have pointed out that her teaching salary—and soon, her temporary income from watching the Plank children—also helped put food on the table. Compared with his provisions over the years, she felt her contribution was meager at best.

"Of course not, *Groossdaadi*," Hannah replied. "I'm sorry you were hungry yesterday. I sliced extra bologna for you today."

Please, Lord, continue to provide my groossdaadi *and me our daily bread*, she prayed as she wrapped a few bread crusts to take to school for lunch. *And allow the loaf to rise big enough to feed Samuel, Sarah and Simon, as well.*

Come sunrise, Sawyer woke the children to get dressed for school. As the boys pulled their shirts over their heads, he noticed how prominent their ribs and shoulder blades were becoming. How had this happened during the few weeks Gertrude was away? It emphasized the need for them to return home and establish their normal routine as soon as possible.

He was grateful his uncle prepared a substantial breakfast of ham and eggs, but it was so early the children hadn't any appetites, especially not for a meal fit for grown men. Sawyer bundled fruit and bread with slices of meat into separate sacks for each of them for lunch. After instructing them to complete their morning chores, he strode to the barn with his cousins.

His body ached as he walked. Farming required him to use a different set of muscles from those he exercised at his cabinetry shop. The leftover stew they'd eaten for dinner the night before sat like a rock in his gut. No wonder the children were unable to finish their portions. As he groaned from the effects of nausea and the stifling morning air, he remembered he needed to discuss the children's dietary needs with Hannah. Yet he couldn't imagine how he might broach the subject or what her reaction would be.

There was something—not necessarily mysterious, nor distrustful, but definitely skittish—about Hannah that caused him to want to measure his words with her. Or at least, that caused him not to want to offend her. Yet he seemed to do exactly that.

The dilemma occupied his mind as he performed the morning chores, and he tried to recall how he and Eliza settled their differences concerning the children. Funny, but he couldn't remember having many. Without speaking about it, they tended to naturally agree on what was best for Simon, Samuel and Sarah. Their mutually shared perspective about raising the children was a strength he missed terribly. Even when they disagreed about some small aspect of the children's care, Eliza's opinion was invaluable to Sawyer and they always reached a reasonable compromise. He wished she were there to guide him about what to do now.

By the time he had hitched up the horse to take the children to school, he concluded being forthright about the sweets was the best approach. Hannah undoubtedly would understand and honor his requests concerning the children, but unless he made them clear, how would she know what they were? After all, she was no Eliza.

Hannah was still so excited about the prospect of becoming a nanny that she hadn't been able to eat when she sat down with her grandfather for breakfast. So when she arrived half an hour early to school, she settled behind her desk and peeled the shell from a hard-boiled egg.

Still trying to come up with inexpensive meals she could make for the children, she realized as long as the chickens were laying, eggs were plentiful, a good source of protein and cost nothing. Likewise, the garden was still going strong with tomatoes and corn, but she brooded about their limited dairy supply, knowing how important milk was for growing children.

When she finished her egg, she smeared a dab of preserves over a crust of bread. She was wiping the corner of her mouth with a napkin when the heavy door inched open.

"*Guder mariye*, Teacher," the triplets said in unison. With their pink cheeks and blond hair backlit by the sun streaming in behind them, they looked positively adorable, and Hannah couldn't help but smile at their appearance.

"Guder mariye," she replied. "Is it just the three of you today, or have you brought your friend, the toad, inside?"

She was referring to the toad they'd caught the previous morning, but as soon as she finished her sentence, Sawyer crossed the threshold.

"Guder mariye," he stated apprehensively. "Might I have a word with you outside?"

She followed him to the landing and squinted up at him. Against the sunshine, he appeared aglow, with the light rimming his strapping shoulders in golden hues and bouncing off his blond curls. But when she noticed his austere expression, she worried he might have thought she was referencing *him* when she'd asked the children about the toad.

"Is something wrong?" she questioned.

"Neh..." Sawyer objected slowly. "But there's something I'd like to bring to your attention."

Hannah thought whatever it was he wanted to discuss, it must have been a grave matter—he could hardly look at her.

"How may I be of assistance?" she asked, hoping to put him at ease.

"You are already of assistance. Perhaps too much so," he began hesitantly. He glanced away and back at her. "It is my understanding that you gave sweet bread and preserves to Simon the other afternoon?"

Oh, then, it wasn't a serious matter at all. He simply wanted to thank her; how kind.

"It was a trifling. I'm happy to share with any child who may be hungry."

"But it wasn't a trifling," Sawyer countered. "It ruined Simon's appetite for more substantial food. I recognize many Amish families consider pastries and other treats to be part of their daily bread—especially in Willow Creek. But, as you probably noticed, my *kinner* are a bit thin and it is important for their physical health that they receive adequate sustenance. I trust the meals you will prepare as part of the *kinner's* daily care will be nutritious and substantial, with limited sweets?"

Hannah felt as if the air had been squeezed from her lungs. Here she had sacrificed her entire noonday meal and Sawyer was acting as if she'd tried to *poison* the boy. She felt at once both foolish and angry, and her face blazed as she struggled to keep her composure.

"Of course," she agreed. "*Kinner*—all *kinner*, whether they are from Pennsylvania or Ohio—do need sustenance, which is why I often bring extra eggs or a slice of meat to school. Two days ago, I had only brought bread enough for me. Your Simon upended the lunch sack into the dirt, so I gave bread and jam to him as well as to Sarah and Samuel. But Simon later complained of a headache and I thought it was because he was still hungry, so I permitted him another piece. But I apologize for ruining his appetite for *adequate sustenance*. I assure you it won't happen again, and I most definitely will prepare healthy recipes while they are under my care."

She stomped up the stairs and into the classroom, leaving Sawyer alone on the stoop.

Sawyer was so abashed, he didn't know whether to follow Hannah and apologize or flee as quickly as he could. As he was hesitating, an approaching buggy caught his eye and he decided to leave.

He tried to shrug off his interaction with her as being an unfortunate misunderstanding, but despite his efforts, throughout the morning he couldn't shake her expression from his mind. She looked as if she'd been stung. And no wonder—he'd been such an oaf, criticizing her when she was only looking after Simon's welfare.

"Are you watching the clouds or napping with your eyes open?" Jonas ribbed him when he drifted into thought.

He wiped his hands on his trousers without saying a word and continued to work. He decided there was only one thing he could do—apologize to Hannah. He needed to be as forthright now as he'd tried to be this morning. He completed his tasks with a new vigor, motivated by his resolve to set things right.

But when he arrived at the schoolhouse, Samuel, Sarah and Simon were playing tag with a girl Sawyer recognized from the first day of school.

"Where is your teacher?" he called to them.

"She's inside, speaking to my wife, Miriam," a voice from behind him answered. The dark-haired man was short and stout. "I'm Jacob Stolzfus and that girl your son is chasing around the willow is my daughter, Abigail. You must be Sawyer Plank, John's nephew."

"I am," Sawyer responded. "Those are my *kinner*, Sarah, Simon and Samuel, the one who just tagged your daughter."

"Abigail has told us about your Sarah," Jacob commented. "She already is very fond of her."

"Sarah is pleased to have a girl her age for a friend, as well," Sawyer acknowledged. "Usually her brothers are her primary playmates. She's happy not to be outnumbered."

As they spoke, the door to the schoolhouse swung open and Miriam and Hannah emerged. Miriam was stroking her swollen belly and chatting animatedly. A breeze played with the strings of Hannah's prayer *kapp*, and Sawyer was distracted by the sight of her lifting a slender hand to cover her bright pink lips, as if to contain a mirthful gasp.

"How about you?" Jacob was saying.

"Pardon?"

"How do you find Willow Creek so far?"

"It's to my liking," he answered absentmindedly, still watching as Miriam and Hannah descended the staircase. "It is unique, to say the least."

"You might consider staying beyond the harvest, since you wouldn't be leaving behind a farm of your own in Ohio," suggested Jacob. "Our district is shrinking. Any relative of John Plank's would be *wilkom* to take up residence here permanently. We could use a young family like yours in our district."

At the bottom step, Hannah glanced up and Sawyer caught her eye. He noticed a slight dimming of her countenance before she continued to amble with Miriam toward their buggy.

"Neh," Sawyer replied definitively. "I am only here for a short while to help my *onkel*, as you apparently have heard. Everything I have is in Ohio—my business, my home, my family. People there depend on me and I on them. It's true I don't own a farm, but the Lord gave me responsibilities there I wouldn't soon abandon."

He sharply called to the triplets, who sprinted across the lawn and piled into the buggy. The children waved to Abigail, her family and Hannah as they rode away, but Sawyer kept his eyes locked on the road ahead of him.

That night when supper was served and they each asked for second helpings—Simon even requested a third—he decided no matter Hannah's reason for feeding his children, he had been right to prohibit her from giving them sweets before supper as a general rule. An apology to her wasn't necessary after all.

Hannah wiped her forehead with the back of her hand. She hoped the hot spell would break, but it still seemed more like the dog days of summer than nearly autumn. She was grateful Jacob and Miriam had given her a ride home from school on their way back from town, but standing over the gas stove cooking supper in the tiny kitchen caused her to sweat almost as much as if she'd walked home.

"It's dry," her grandfather said disgustedly about the chicken she'd prepared. "Bring me a different piece."

Since she had served the only meat they had, Hannah took both of their plates to the stove and covertly switched her piece with his, slicing off the ends so he wouldn't notice. While her back was still turned toward him, she practiced an old trick she and Eve sometimes used to communicate with each other.

"Just once I wish I had someone to talk to in the evening who had something pleasant to say." She spoke aloud, knowing he couldn't see to read her lips. "Either that, or I wish *I* were the one who was deaf, so I couldn't hear your surly remarks."

Without Eve's sympathetic ear, expressing herself in such a manner did little to defuse Hannah's frustration, and she remained feisty until bedtime, rushing through her evening prayers before crawling into bed. She kicked off her sheets as a drop of perspiration trickled down the side of her cheek and into her ear. Or perhaps it was a tear. Despite her best efforts to please everyone, the day had been plagued with upsetting events.

First, Sawyer had shamed her for sharing her bread with Simon. Then Miriam had shown up at the schoolhouse at the end of the day and her effervescent glee emphasized how bereft Hannah felt.

Although Amish women were reluctant to discuss such matters—sometimes not even mentioning they were carrying a child until the baby was born—Miriam confided that earlier in the morning, she had consulted a midwife.

"I'll soon give birth to a healthy *bobbel*, *Gott* willing," Miriam tearfully divulged. "After losing three unborn *bobblin*, I can't tell you how joyful we are."

"I am very joyful for you," Hannah said, squeezing Miriam's arm. "I will keep you in my prayers."

"*Denki.* The midwife warned me that meanwhile I must limit my physical activities. Abigail is a help, but with her at school, it's difficult for me to keep up the house and garden."

Judging from how full-figured Miriam had become, Hannah guessed she had merely a month or two before she delivered, but that was an unspoken subject, something only God knew for certain.

She was truly glad for Miriam and Jacob, and she wouldn't have dreamed of begrudging them such fulfillment. Nor did she envy Miriam's marriage: she'd always known Jacob wasn't the Lord's intended for her. But Miriam's news made her all the more aware that soon she'd have to bid her students goodbye—and teaching them was the closest she'd ever come to having *kinner* herself. What was she going to do without their daily presence in her life?

It didn't help that just as Miriam was telling her about the *bobbel*, Hannah glimpsed Sawyer conversing with Jacob, and his chastisement burned afresh in her mind. It almost seemed as if neither man nor God believed she was fit to care for children!

Her hurt was further magnified by the letter she had received upon arriving home.

Dearest Hannah, her sister's familiar penmanship said. *I am so ecstatic I will burst if I have to keep it to myself any longer: I am with child!*

Of course, Hannah was elated that God had provided such a blessing for Eve, and she was exuberant she would soon be an aunt. But her joy was tinged with envy. Not only had her sister managed—at twenty-four years of age, which was considered late in life by their district's standards—to meet and marry a good man who thoroughly loved her, but soon she'd experience motherhood, too.

Every time Hannah thought she'd finally accepted that her prime responsibility was to care for her grandfather and her life wouldn't include marriage or children, the desire for both manifested itself again, like symptoms of a virus she couldn't shake. Would she ever be cured of the longing to have what it seemed she wasn't meant to? *And why can't I have it?* she lamented. It wasn't as if she longed for something sinful: the Bible described children and married life as being gifts from God.

She eased out of bed, donned her prayer *kapp* and knelt in the darkness. *Please, Lord, show me Your provision for my life, especially once my teaching job ends*, she beseeched. *And help me to be content with it, whatever it may be.*

When she awoke the next morning, her pillow was still damp and her eyes were swollen, but her spirit was inexplicably peaceful. She didn't know how it would happen, but she did know one way or another, God would provide for all of her physical, emotional and spiritual needs. She donned her *kapp* and knelt again.

Lord, please forgive my envy and lack of faith. Help me to spend this day in glad service to You, she prayed.

Despite the heat, she felt refreshed as she hiked through the fields toward the schoolhouse, listening to the birds and inhaling the scent of wildflowers. After Sawyer's visit the previous morning, she had distanced herself from Sarah, Simon and Samuel for the rest of the day, fearing their father might interpret any kind attention she paid to them as spoiling them.

But this morning, she realized she hadn't responded maturely to Sawyer's misunderstanding or given him a chance to acknowledge his mistake. She saw why he was concerned about his children's health, and she'd certainly respect his wishes regarding their diet. As long as she didn't give them treats, she didn't believe he'd fault her for being nurturing and warm.

The thought of a treat caused her mouth to water. Yesterday she was so out of sorts that she barely swallowed five bites of supper, and suddenly she felt ravenous. When she reached the classroom, she unwrapped a piece of sweet bread from her bag and pulled the preserves from the cooler. She bit into a thick slice, closing her eyes to enjoy the flavor in quiet solitude.

"*Guder mariye*, Teacher," several small voices squeaked merrily, interrupting her thoughts.

Her mouth was too full to reply, but she reflexively stashed the remaining food into her bag, embarrassed to be caught eating at her desk again.

"Guder mariye," Sawyer echoed his children.

Hannah chewed quickly and then swallowed before replying. *"Guder mariye."*

"Is that the bread your *groossmammi* learned you how to make?" Samuel pointed.

"*Teached* you," Sarah corrected. "And it's not polite to point."

"Hush," Sawyer instructed them both. "We disrupted your teacher's breakfast. *Kumme*, we'll wait outside until she is finished."

"*Denki*, but I wasn't really eating," Hannah protested.

Sawyer noticed a smudge of preserves at the corner of her mouth. She must have sensed him looking at it, because she traced her lips with her finger, her cheeks blotching with color.

"I mean, I wasn't eating breakfast," she faltered. "It was only a treat. I have eggs for breakfast. Sometimes ham. That is, despite what you may think, I don't ordinarily just have treats for breakfast. Or for snacks. Or at any time of the day. Not every day, anyway, or not without eating something else, as well. But I was terribly hungry, you see, because—"

"I am terribly hungry, too," Sawyer interrupted. His resolve not to apologize suddenly dissipated, and he felt nothing but a desire to ease Hannah's discomfort, which he knew he had caused with his comments the day before. "The *kinner* are hungry, as well. Last night, my *onkel's* dinner sat like bricks in our bellies, so this morning we were unable to eat breakfast. What we wouldn't do for a piece of bread and strawberry preserves..."

Cocking her head to one side, Hannah narrowed her eyes at him for what seemed an interminable pause. Rather than speaking, she again removed the jar of preserves from the cooler and pulled the bread apart in chunks. After spooning a dollop onto each piece, she directed the triplets to eat theirs at their desks. She gave the biggest piece to Sawyer, who stood next to her while he devoured it.

When he was finished, he wiped his mouth with the back of his hand. "I must apologize," he began. "I fear I misjudged you."

"Say no more. I accept your apology." She smiled readily. Then she asked, "Are your *onkel's* meals really like bricks in your bellies?"

"Unfortunately, they are. In fact, I have a hunch Simon dropped their lunch bag on purpose. I know I would have, if it meant I'd get to eat a piece of your sweet bread instead."

Hannah's giggle reminded him of a wind chime. "It tastes alright, then?"

"Better than a dream," Sawyer replied.

Hannah's face again flushed. "That's a kind thing for you to say," she replied modestly and busied herself putting the lid on the jar before meeting his eyes again.

"I want you to know I *do* understand and respect your concerns about your *kinner's* health," she said somberly. "I have noticed they are thin, but it's possible they're going through a growth spurt, and their width hasn't caught up with their height yet. In any case, in Willow Creek, we like to think our *gut* farm air has a way of working up healthy appetites, and I'll feed those appetites with wholesome, hearty suppers."

Sawyer blinked and ran his hands over his head, pushing back his curls. Until that instant, he hadn't realized how much he'd needed reassurance that the children would be alright. He was so often in the position of instructing and comforting his children, encouraging Gertrude and guiding his crew at work that he rarely received a word of consolation himself. Her sentiment was as heartening as something Eliza may have said, and he was touched. His silence allowed Hannah to continue speaking.

"My intention is to help relieve your concerns, Sawyer, not to add to them. I hope you won't worry about Simon, Sarah and Samuel while they're under my care. But if you have a concern, please tell me—I promise not to have another tantrum like a *kind* myself, as I did yesterday."

Sawyer broke into a huge grin. "Hannah Lantz," he replied, "you may be slight in stature, but you most certainly are no child!"

When Hannah looked perplexed, he rushed to explain, "I mean that you're every bit a woman."

Her forehead and cheeks went pink and her eyes widened. Clearly he was embarrassing her.

"An adult, that is," Sawyer clarified. "Someone I wholeheartedly trust to mind my *kinner*."

As he stood there feeling every bit the fool, two boys shuffled up the stairs into the classroom.

"*Guder mariye*, Caleb and Eli," Hannah greeted them. To Sawyer she said, "Those are friends of Samuel and Simon's."

"Ah, Caleb, whose bloody mouth you tended to—the *kinner* told me about it."

"High drama in the school yard," Hannah said with a giggle, and Sawyer knew any awkwardness between them had passed. "It's all in a day's work."

"Speaking of work," Sawyer remembered, "I should be going now."

"Me, too." Hannah nodded. "I hope you have a pleasant day."

The day was already far more pleasant than Sawyer could have hoped for himself.

Chapter Four

"Be careful!" Hannah's grandfather commanded as she helped him hoist the dollhouse into the buggy Saturday morning. "This could fetch a pretty penny, but not if you crack it."

Hannah dismissed his harsh admonishment as concern about their income. The dollhouse was larger and more detailed than any he'd ever made before—clearly he had designed it to appeal to *Englisch* tourists—so it was no wonder he wanted to be certain it arrived without a nick. She mopped her brow and took her place beside him in the buggy, uttering a silent prayer for travel mercies.

As they sped past the fields and into town, Hannah let her mind wander to her conversation with Sawyer, as it had often done in the past hours, making light work of wringing and hanging the clothes and scrubbing the floors. *Better than a dream*, he had said about her sweet bread. She knew pride was a sin, but being given a compliment was such a rare occurrence she couldn't help but treasure his words. They weren't merely flattery, either—his bright green eyes had shone with genuine earnestness as he'd spoken the phrase.

A driver honked his horn, jarring Hannah from her thoughts. She touched her grandfather's sleeve to warn him of the approaching vehicle so he could move to the shoulder of the road, but he jerked his arm away. She was relieved when they finally pulled into the lane behind the mercantile. So many tourists' cars filled the lot that Hannah and her grandfather had to tie their horse at the designated horse and buggy plot nearly a quarter of a mile away.

They purchased their groceries and returned to the buggy to secure them there before heading to Schrock's Shop, which was located three doors down from the mercantile. Hannah helped her grandfather unload the dollhouse first; they'd come back to retrieve the other toys later. She was aware of but not bothered by the curious stares of the *Englischers* as they trudged down the long street toward the shop.

Hannah's grandfather had been apprenticed as a carpenter—he once owned a small furniture shop that eventually closed for lack of business. After that, he reluctantly went to work in the *Englisch*-run factory on the edge of town. Ever since the company retired him some eight years ago, he had been consigning wooden toys at Schrock's, where his work was highly prized among tourists. Eve's quilts were equally appreciated. However, sometimes it seemed the *Englisch* were willing to *praise* more than they were willing to *pay*, so the income generated from the sales was nominal at best.

Still, the sales had been a provision from the Lord, and Hannah thought about how thankful she was for that as she pulled open the door to the back entrance.

"Guder nammidaag," she said, wishing a good afternoon to Joseph Schrock, Daniel Schrock's son, who was in charge of making consignment arrangements for new merchandise.

He looked up from where he was sitting at his desk, a pinched expression on his face. "Good afternoon, Hannah, Albert," he greeted them in *Englisch.*

As they placed the dollhouse carefully on the floor,

Hannah expected Joseph to fuss over it more than he usually did, since the dollhouse was especially handsome. Instead, Joseph slid his pencil behind his ear and offered them a chair.

Her grandfather refused. “I am not so old I need to sit after a stroll down the lane.”

Hannah’s cheeks grew hot, but out of respect for her grandfather, she remained standing, too. Joseph excused himself to close the door leading to the main gallery where the customers browsed.

“The news isn’t good, Albert,” Joseph acknowledged. He mouthed the words toward Hannah’s grandfather, but his eyes shifted to Hannah. He held up two fingers. “Only two of your items sold since you were last here. The *Englisch* are less inclined to buy wooden toys any longer. They spend their money on electronic devices, I am told.”

Hannah chewed her lip, nodding.

“I’m afraid we have to limit the amount of shelf space we can devote to your items, Albert. Until what you have here already sells, we cannot accept more toys. Especially not something as large as that dollhouse.”

Hannah’s grandfather pounded his fist against the desktop, causing Hannah and Joseph both to jump.

“I made the cradle you slept in, Joseph Schrock!” he shouted. “Your own sons have slept in it, as well. Now, are you to tell me you’re turning away my goods?”

“My father made the decision, and it is final,” Joseph stated, nervously pushing his glasses from where they’d slid down the bridge of his nose.

“What is final,” Hannah’s grandfather thundered, “is that we will never darken your doorstep again!”

He grunted as he bent to heave the dollhouse from the floor, and Hannah leaped to his aid.

"I'm sorry," Joseph apologized to her. "I hope you understand."

Hannah felt pulled between being loyal to her grandfather and being polite to Joseph. She dipped her head so her grandfather wouldn't see her lips move but replied in their German dialect so Joseph would remember whom he was dealing with. "*Mach's gut*, Joseph."

Although he spent Saturday morning working in the fields with his cousins, Sawyer cut his work short to take a trip into town in the afternoon for groceries. John was learning to navigate around the house on his crutches and to provide minimal assistance on the farm, but he still couldn't climb into and out of the buggy without another adult helping him. Rather than having two adults make the trip, Sawyer volunteered to go.

Samuel, Sarah and Simon were apt contributors to the daily chores around the house and with the farm animals. The boys also wanted to participate however they could in the fields, but Sawyer's cousins generally treated them more like hindrances than helpers, and often sent them on errands to fetch tools that were impossibly heavy for the boys to carry on their own. Sawyer thought it best to keep the children from being underfoot.

He also figured by doing the shopping he'd have a bit of input into what kind of meals John prepared for breakfast and dinner. But his main objective was to stock up on staples for Hannah and her grandfather, who surely weren't equipped to feed three more mouths.

Sawyer and the children were toting packages toward their buggy when Simon hooted, "Look, there's Teacher!"

Across the street, an old man and Hannah were struggling to lug a cumbersome object along the sidewalk.

"They have a dollhouse!" Sarah marveled.

"Kumme," Sawyer directed. "Follow closely."

He led them across the street through a clearing in traffic.

"Hannah," he beckoned. "Hannah Lantz!"

She came to a halt but the old man continued, nearly losing his balance. The dollhouse teetered between them. Sawyer dropped his parcels where he stood and lunged to steady their burden.

"Please, allow me," he said as he deftly pulled the dollhouse to his chest. In the process, his arm brushed Hannah's, and heat rose to his face. The touch was unintended, but he hoped she didn't think his gesture was impudent or resent him for interfering.

"Denki," she replied and greeted the children, but she didn't introduce the old man, who had pivoted and swooped up Sawyer's packages from the sidewalk.

"My sons can carry those," Sawyer began to say, but the man walked on without acknowledging him.

"My *groossdaadi* is deaf," Hannah reminded him quietly, so the children wouldn't hear. "He is also stubborn, so please let him carry the bags. We are just down there, on the other side of the lot."

Sawyer nodded and they continued walking side by side. In his peripheral vision, he noticed her expression was so forlorn, he wondered if she was ill. Was this the same woman whose lilting laughter had filled the schoolroom only days before? He tried to think of something conversational to say, but he drew a blank.

At the buggy, Hannah's grandfather handed the packages to the boys and Sawyer helped him secure the dollhouse into the back. The old man untied the horse from the far end of the hitching rail and repositioned the carriage. Then he climbed inside next to Hannah and took the reins in his hands.

Only then did he pause to acknowledge Sawyer, who looked him squarely in the eye and enunciated exaggeratedly, “I am Sawyer Plank, whose *kinner* Hannah will be caring for after school.”

“Albert Lantz,” the man yelled back.

“That is high-quality workmanship,” Sawyer stated, nodding toward the dollhouse.

“Hmpff,” the man snorted, but his eyes seemed to brighten.

“Your granddaughter Hannah is a fine teacher,” Sawyer said. “The *kinner*—”

But before he could finish his sentence, the old man broke eye contact and slapped the reins against the horse’s back.

“Giddy up!” he shouted, and Sawyer hopped back, his legs buckling beneath him as the wheels rolled forward and the buggy pulled away.

Hannah clenched her fists on her lap, fighting back tears. It was bad enough that her grandfather had demonstrated such an unbridled temper to Joseph Schrock, but he had been deliberately rude to Sawyer Plank, as well.

Joseph knew what her grandfather was like, but Sawyer met him only today. Perhaps Sawyer might have believed her grandfather didn’t hear the words he spoke, but there was no mistaking the fact that her grandfather nearly rolled over his foot with the buggy! Why did he behave that way, especially toward someone who was being as helpful as Sawyer was?

By the time they returned home, carried the dollhouse back to his workshop and Hannah had set supper on the table, her grandfather’s mood seemed to have lightened. Hannah’s burden, however, had intensified, as she wondered how to stretch out their meals. If only her grandfather hadn't left the store in such haste—they hadn't collected what was due them from the two toys that sold, and they desperately needed the money.

"You are not eating?" he asked when Hannah took only a scant amount of pork and sauerkraut.

"The heat," she mouthed simply, waving her hand in the air to indicate the warm weather even though she doubted it was the humidity that tied her stomach up in knots.

"I'll have another helping," he ordered, thrusting the dish toward Hannah.

She knew his request meant he enjoyed the food more than usual, and she served him an ample scoop. At least the next day she wouldn't have to worry about providing their dinner, since they'd eat following church service. She only needed to be certain to have a light meal on hand in the event they received unexpected visitors for Sunday night supper, as was the practice in their district.

After she dried the last dish, she sat adjacent to her grandfather, who was silently reading the weekly newspaper, *The Budget*. Out of the corner of her eye, Hannah could see the man's profile fringed by the gray of his sideburns and beard. His lips moved as he read to himself, and she was instantly filled with compassion.

She supposed the way he saw it, the shopkeeper's son might as well have told him his life's work was meaningless. Her grandfather once had a reputation for being one of the most skilled furniture makers in the district, and now he couldn't even peddle his toys to *Englisch* tourists, who weren't exactly esteemed for their eye for craftsmanship.

He was old, deaf and near penniless, and she realized he deserved more respect than certain people—including herself, if only in her thoughts—had given him. Hadn't he raised her and provided for her all these years? And didn't she know how troubling it was to feel as if you'd lost your purpose? She might have lashed out the same way if she were in his shoes.

Before folding back her sheets that night, she silently prayed, asking God to forgive her own anger and allow her to mend the rift with Joseph Schrock her grandfather had created by his. She ended by asking once again, *And please, Lord, give us our daily bread.*

"Daed, Daed!" screamed Sarah.

Before his eyes were even open, Sawyer leaped out of bed and scrambled for her room. He propelled himself forward so quickly that he slipped and crashed against the door. He managed to brace himself against the frame with his hands, but not before his forehead made contact with the knob.

I'm getting hit at both ends today, he thought as he staggered down the hall.

"Hush, Sarah, hush," he quieted her. "It's only a dream."

"Giant black horses were circling me," she cried. "I was all alone. I kept calling you and calling you, but you couldn't hear me."

"I am here now," he said soothingly. "I heard you calling me and I came. But you must remember, the Lord is always with you, so you are never truly alone."

After Sarah finally dropped back to sleep, Sawyer stretched out in his bed and put his arms behind his head, which by that time was throbbing from his fall. It was little surprise that Sarah had such a vivid dream; the day had been filled with unpleasant experiences.

First, she had witnessed him narrowly springing clear of Albert Lantz's buggy, only to land on his backside. His dignity had been the only part of him that was injured, but the near-accident frightened Sarah to tears.

Then, an hour after dinner, Sarah and Samuel were

both sick to their stomachs. The only reason Simon didn't throw up was because he barely took two small bites of the undercooked fish John served, filling up instead on potatoes and broccoli.

"When my brother and I were their age, we ate what our *mamm* served or we went to bed hungry," Jonas said gruffly, and Sawyer hadn't pointed out that their mother's cooking was undoubtedly better than their dad's.

Rubbing his eyes, he prayed, *Lord, please help Sarah to sleep through the night.* When he took his hand away, his fingers felt sticky. He realized he'd broken his skin during the fall and knew he should get up to rinse it off, but before he could give it a second thought, he drifted into dreamland himself. The next thing he knew, it was time to rise and milk the cows before church services.

"What happened to you?" Phillip asked as they headed to the barn in the light from the rising sun.

"I tripped in the dark last night and whacked my head on the doorknob."

"You're as clumsy as the boys," Jonas ridiculed. "I heard the ruckus and assumed they were horsing around."

Sawyer counted to three so he wouldn't respond defensively. Although the boys engaged in horseplay during the day, they'd never been disruptive of anyone's sleep, so Jonas had no reason to suspect they caused the late-night commotion.

"*Neh*, it was me. Sarah had another nightmare, so I was rushing to her room when I fell."

"If you ask me," Jonas advised, "she shouldn't be so afraid of her own shadow by now. She's a *scholar*, not a *bobbel*."

Sawyer didn't know how to take Jonas's remark. Perhaps he and Phillip weren't used to the ways of small children because they didn't have younger siblings. Or, because it had been several years since Lydia died, maybe they couldn't remember how their *mamm* nurtured them when they were youngsters.

That was yet another reason he appreciated Gertrude's—and now Hannah's—presence in the children's lives: he wanted them to have a maternal influence, especially Sarah. Sawyer knew how to raise boys, but girls were a different matter. Still, he wondered if Jonas was right and he was being too soft. Eliza would have known better what to expect of a girl Sarah's age.

He changed the subject, teasing his cousins about a topic he knew was at the forefront of their teenage minds.

"I'm looking forward to the services today," he said. "I want to see if it's true, that there are no young women in Willow Creek to capture your fancy. Although, Jonas, if you usually show up wearing that scowl on your face, it's no wonder they go into hiding."

Jonas joked back, "The sight of your forehead is the only thing that would make a woman go into hiding, *dopplich*!"

Sawyer didn't mind his cousin calling him clumsy. "*Kumme*, we'd both better wash the 'ugly' from our faces, then," he agreed, affectionately clapping Jonas on the shoulder as they headed back to the house to get ready for church.

That Sunday, services were held at Miriam and Jacob Stolzfus's home. Afterward Sawyer surveyed the young women setting the long, makeshift lunch tables the men had set up in the yard. Most of the females wore black *kapps* to church, indicating they were unmarried, but they appeared so young as to be children themselves.

He was just thinking he could understand why Jonas attended singings in a neighboring district when he spotted the black *kapp* of a *maedel* delivering a pitcher of water to a freshly set table. From behind, Sawyer couldn't distinguish her age for certain—she was small enough to be a teenager but something about her posture suggested the poise of an adult.

He craned his neck to peer over a row of men taking their places at the table. The woman glanced over her shoulder at that moment and Sawyer recognized it was Hannah. His pulse quickened when she gave him the briefest of nods before turning forward again.

He'd have to wait for her to finish serving before telling her he'd bought a surplus of items for her pantry so she wouldn't worry about having three extra mouths to feed in the coming weeks. Just as she didn't want their arrangement to add to Sawyer's concerns, he didn't want it to add to hers. But meanwhile, when he spotted Hannah's grandfather voraciously wolfing down a helping of bread, cold slices of ham, cheese and pickled beets, he deliberately took a seat at the farthest end of the table. He already had two bumps too many to risk getting a third.

Although lunch at the women's table was a rushed affair—everyone knew there were more people after them waiting for a seat, so they ate quickly and then vacated the space—Hannah welcomed the opportunity to visit with the other ladies afterward while they did dishes.

"Have you heard the news?" Doris Hooley hissed, nodding toward Miriam.

"You mean about Miriam being with child?" Hannah asked, realizing she was spoiling Doris's gossip. She was surprised Miriam had confided in Doris, too, but perhaps she was too exuberant to exercise prudence. "Isn't it *wunderbaar*?"

"Jah," Doris agreed and directed her next question to Miriam. "Did you know that John Plank has a nephew vis-

iting for harvest season? We have a wealthy widower in our midst—and he is six foot two if he's an inch!"

"His name is Sawyer Plank," Hannah confirmed to Miriam. "He was chatting with Jacob when you visited the schoolhouse recently."

"I think I recall seeing him," Miriam said. "My Abigail talks about his Sarah incessantly. They've become fast friends. She enjoys his sons, as well."

"*Jah*, they're all very eager scholars and—"

"Enough talk about the *kinner*," Doris interrupted. "Let's talk about their *daed*. I found him to act a bit stiff initially, but perhaps he's the silent, brooding type. He needs a little loosening up. Hannah, you've had many conversations with him. What do you think?"

Hannah was so flabbergasted by Doris's assessment that she didn't know quite how to respond. "I hold him in high regard as the *daed* of my students."

Doris rolled her eyes and commented to Miriam, "She has to say something formal like that—he's also her employer. She's taking care of his *kinner* after school."

"That's not true!" Hannah protested.

"You're not caring for his *kinner* after school?" Doris smirked mischievously.

"I think what Hannah means," Miriam interjected, "is that her primary focus is on her scholars, not on their *daed*, even though she finds him to be a very decent man."

Hannah shot her a grateful look, but Miriam's words were wasted on Doris, who retorted, "Well, while you're focusing on the *kinner*, I'm going to focus on Sawyer. I would have thought that someone in your financial situation would have been leaping to stake a more, shall we say, *permanent arrangement* with him. But if not, just don't complain that I didn't give you every opportunity. You, of all people, should know not to let an eligible bachelor pass you by, lest someone else snatch him up."

Hannah was doubly embarrassed. First, because Doris drew attention to how strapped she was financially and implied that Hannah would use Sawyer to improve her future status. Secondly, Doris's remarks included a direct reference to Hannah's rejection of Jacob, and she felt so mortified that Doris had brought up the subject after all these years that she couldn't even look at Miriam.

"Excuse me, please. I'm finished here and I need some air," Hannah calmly stated, wringing out the dishcloth.

She found a quiet place in the yard beneath an apple tree. Picking up a stray piece of fruit, she rubbed it against her skirt and paced in small circles. There was a third reason for Hannah's agitation: it annoyed her that Doris was intent on pursuing Sawyer.

It wasn't that Hannah had a romantic interest in him herself, but she resented how easy Doris assumed it would be to win his affections and perhaps even become his wife. Or perhaps she resented the fact that in Doris's case, marriage *could* have been simply a matter of falling in love and getting wed; Doris had no other responsibilities or obstacles standing in her way. Even her advanced age didn't seem to discourage her. Hannah supposed she could have drawn inspiration from her friend's attitude, but on this roasting afternoon, she just felt irritated.

The longer she waited for her grandfather to finish his meal, the more agitated she became, and she was so consumed by her own impatience that when she heard her name called from behind, she twitched, dropping the apple.

"I'm sorry—I didn't mean to startle you," Sawyer said.

He had been trying to remember to use a softer tone, especially around Hannah, but he had been so keen to talk to her, he couldn't contain his eagerness. He bent to pick up the fruit that had rolled toward his feet. Before straightening to his full height, he noticed she avoided meeting his eyes, and he thought she was angry at him for his trespass. Had she been praying? Did she wish to have a quiet moment alone?

"Better a bruised apple than a bruised foot," she said, her fingertips grazing his as she accepted the fruit. She seemed almost embarrassed to look at him.

"Pardon me?" he questioned. She was so quick-witted that he sometimes was puzzled by her turns of phrase.

"I mean, I am the one who is sorry. Please accept my apology for my *groossdaadi's* reckless steering yesterday."

Sawyer waved his hand in dismissal. "Your grandfather was concentrating on the horse, not on me. I shouldn't have been standing so close to the wheel. After all, he is deaf."

"Deaf, *jah*, but blind, *neh*." Hannah's white smile brightened her face, and when she finally peeked upward at him, she gasped. "Oh, *neh*! Your forehead! Was that from yester—"

Sawyer's hand flew to his eyebrow. He'd forgotten all about it. *"Neh,"* he assured her. "Your *groossdaadi* may be a poor driver, but I am even a worse sleepwalker. I got this when I collided with a doorknob trying to comfort Sarah last night. She has nightmares, you see."

"How upsetting," she commented, scrunching her forehead.

"Some people think I should let her calm herself at night. They say she's too old to be so frightened by her dreams."

"Nonsense!" Hannah declared. "I recall suffering from terrifying dreams after my *mamm* and *daed* died when I was a child. They worsened again when *Groossmammi* passed, and during other times of adjustment. Sarah is fortunate to have you to comfort her. She'll outgrow the nightmares in due time."

Once again, Sawyer found Hannah's insights to be reassuring. He was about to thank her for her encouragement when she added comically, "Of course, you might want to wear your hat into her bedroom at night, lest you scare her all the more with that wounded forehead of yours."

Their laughter was interrupted by Doris's shrill voice.

"Yoo-hoo," she called. "I hear there's a patient in need of nursing."

She waved a vial and cloth as she promenaded in their direction.

"Hello, Sawyer. Jonas told me you had an accident."

"Did he, now?" Sawyer grimaced. "It's nothing, really."

"I'll be the judge of that," Doris ordered. "Here, let me clean it off with witch hazel."

Sawyer put his hands up defensively as Doris approached. No woman had tended to his wounds or touched his face since Eliza died.

Suddenly a man bellowed from the distance, "Hannah! Hannah!"

"I must go. I'll see you both in the morning, *Gott* willing." Hannah excused herself before Sawyer had the chance to mention the groceries.

"Why must you flinch?" Doris chastised. "You're a big strong man, not a *bobbel*, so stop squirming. This won't hurt a bit."

As she dabbed witch hazel onto Sawyer's skin, he closed his eyes and clenched his teeth. Why was it that his conversations with Hannah never lasted nearly as long as he wanted them to, but his interactions with Doris never ended quickly enough?

Chapter Five

Hannah was writing on the blackboard when Sawyer and the children arrived the next morning.

"*Guder mariye*, Hannah," Sawyer said, remembering to subdue his voice.

She turned to face them, her eyes crinkling at the corners. "*Guder mariye*, Sawyer. *Guder mariye*, Simon, Sarah and Samuel."

"Guder mariye," they chorused.

Each of the children approached her desk, gingerly piling it with the sacks they carried, and then scooted outside to play before the other students arrived. Sawyer placed his two larger sacks on the floor.

"What is this?" she asked in surprise.

"It's for your pantry. I realize your travel into town is limited, and I doubt you had time to shop for enough food for three extra mouths."

"Denki," Hannah voiced aloud to Sawyer and then paused to express her silent gratitude to the Lord for His answer to her prayers.

Sawyer quickly said, "I hope you don't receive these supplemental items as an insult—I'm not suggesting you prepare any meals in particular."

"*Neh*, not at all. It's very thoughtful." Amused, she confessed, "But I must say, it looks like enough to fill a silo."

Sawyer chuckled at himself. "My sister Gertrude is the

one who manages our purchases. I admit I never pay much attention to the ingredients she buys."

Hannah faltered. "Nothing will go to waste. It's just..."

"Just what?"

"It's just I haven't brought a wheelbarrow to carry it home in," she said with a giggle.

Sawyer threw back his head, laughing aloud. "I suppose I will have to return this afternoon to give you a ride home, then."

Hannah protested that if he came back in the afternoon, it would disrupt his farmwork and defeat the purpose of her watching the children, but he insisted.

"Just this once won't cause a hardship," he asserted. "It would be my pleasure. Truly."

After Sawyer uttered the words, Hannah remained silent, weighing the situation. Her grandfather wouldn't accept groceries from another man, even though she couldn't possibly stretch their menu without the supplemental food. She didn't want him being rude to Sawyer again, but she supposed there was nothing she could do to stop him.

"It would be my pleasure to accept," she finally stated. "*Denki*, Sawyer. I will see you this afternoon, *Gott* willing."

Although she had intended to show the children the hidden bird's nest she'd spotted near the stream on the shortcut home, Hannah was just as glad to be traversing in the buggy. The hot and humid weather still hadn't broken, and the sun beat down on her shoulders. She caught a faint whiff of Sawyer's sweat, which was mingled with the scent of soap and freshly pitched hay. Watching Sawyer's masculine hands loosely holding the reins made her aware of how rarely she'd been in such close proximity to any man except her grandfather.

She needn't have worried about her grandfather's reaction to receiving the groceries, since he was still in his workshop when they arrived home and Sawyer left promptly after carrying the items to the pantry. She shelved them quickly and then devoted her attention to showing the children around the house and small yard.

"After your chores, you may climb the trees, pick the fruit and play games on the lawn," she said, sweeping her hand expansively. "But," she cautioned seriously, waving one finger, "you mustn't disturb my *groossdaadi* or go near his workshop in the backyard."

"Jah." Samuel nodded seriously. "We must mind our manners and obey whatever you tell us, just as we would at school. *Daed* said so."

"Did he?" Hannah asked. While she appreciated Sawyer's instructions, she wanted the children to feel at home. "Well, your *daed* is right. We should always mind our manners. But that's not exactly why you can't go back to the workshop."

"Then why can't we?" Simon asked.

"Because my *groossdaadi* is working very hard and needs to concentrate. If he is distracted, his hands could slip. He could cut himself or ruin what he is making."

"Did he make the big dollhouse?" Sarah asked.

"*Jah*, he did," Hannah admitted. "He makes toys of all sorts."

"But you're too old for toys!" Samuel exclaimed.

"She is not!" Sarah argued, holding her hands on her hips. "Remember when she batted the ball at school? It went farther than anyone's, even the oldest boys."

"You aren't minding your manners, Sarah," Samuel corrected her. "You're raising your voice. You'll disturb the *groossdaadi*."

"There, there," Hannah said, clapping her hands together twice to break up their argument. "It's true—the toys aren't for me, as much as I sometimes like to bat a ball. My *groossdaadi* sells the toys to *Englischers* in town. And while we shouldn't raise our voices in anger, my *groossdaadi* couldn't hear us if we did. You see, he is deaf."

All three children looked at her, their eyes as big as coins. Their bewilderment was so innocent, she had the urge to pull them onto her lap and give them the tightest squeeze. Instead, she said, "So it is especially important we don't make sudden movements around him, because he can't hear us approaching. It might frighten him."

"Like sneaking up on a wild animal in the woods," Simon said knowingly.

"*Jah*, a little like that." Hannah nodded, amazed by how accurate the boy's metaphor was. "Yet, although my *groossdaadi* can't hear, he can read lips. If you look at him when you are speaking, he can usually tell what you are saying. He can talk back to you, although sometimes he'll use a loud voice. It might sound as if he's yelling or as if he's angry, but he's not. He just can't hear how loud his own voice is."

"*Daed* uses his big voice sometimes," Sarah confided. "But he says he doesn't mean to. He just forgets. Your *groossdaadi* probably just forgets, too."

"*Jah*, he probably does," Hannah agreed, so grateful for the girl's compassion that this time she did sweep the children into a tight squeeze.

Hannah was in a rocker on the porch, reading to the children, when Sawyer pulled up that evening. Their hands and faces were scrubbed, Sarah's hair was neatly combed, and they seemed content, if not sleepy. On the way home, they highlighted the afternoon's adventures for him.

"We climbed to the top of the apple tree to pick the five biggest apples we could find," Samuel reported.

"Hannah showed me how to bake them," Sarah said, glowing. "We added a pinch of sugar and a dusting of cinnamon to the top. Those are measurements every baker must know, she told me."

After tucking them into bed, Sawyer retreated early to his own room. His back was aching and he was exhausted, but he grinned from ear to ear; he'd never heard his children as excited about doing chores like baking or picking apples as they'd been when they were doing them for Hannah.

Denki, *Lord, for how well the* kinner *are adjusting to another change in their lives*, he prayed before easing into bed. *And please keep Sarah from upsetting dreams.* The girl slept soundly through the night without any disturbances, even though a thunderstorm rattled the windows shortly after midnight, and another one blew through right before the break of day.

By the time the children piled into the buggy, the sun had burned off the haze and the day promised to be another scorcher. Still, he was surprised by how withered Hannah looked when he accompanied the children to the classroom door. The dark circles under her eyes intensified their hue, but she appeared heavy-lidded.

"Are you feeling ill?" he inquired.

She looked at him askance, in the familiar manner he'd come to recognize meant she was about to jest. "Do you think I look ill?"

He hadn't meant it like that. "Not at all," he explained. "Just a little tired. I'm afraid one afternoon and evening with my *kinner* may have worn you out completely."

"On the contrary," she protested. "They are one of the most refreshing parts of my day! The thunderstorms kept me awake, which is probably why I'm bleary-eyed. But I am perfectly healthy and my sleepiness will pass. In a few minutes, I'll be as *gut* as new."

"You already are as *gut* as new," Sawyer said without thinking. Then he clarified, "I mean, you needn't apologize for your appearance. That is, your appearance is fine, just fine. Not *just* fine. *Very* fine, I mean. Your appearance is nice. And healthy. Your appearance is healthy."

The more he spoke, the more his ears burned and the more perplexed Hannah's expression grew. He had the sensation of sprinting down a hill; the momentum of his own words was causing him to trip all over himself. He wondered what Eliza might have thought if she had been there to hear his gibberish.

Fortunately, at that moment, Jacob Stolzfus ascended the stairs. "*Guder mariye*, Sawyer," he said. "Hannah, might I have a word with you?"

"Absolutely," Hannah agreed, relief filling her voice. "I'll see you this evening, Sawyer."

Sawyer couldn't get away from the schoolhouse fast enough. What had come over him? He worked the horse into a galloping clip, as if he were trying to outpace his own embarrassment.

"Did I interrupt an argument? Was Sawyer Plank being rude to you?" Jacob Stolzfus asked protectively.

Hannah quickly denied it. "Sawyer has never been anything but polite and kind to me."

"You were both red in the face," Jacob persisted.

"This weather could make anyone's skin flush," Hannah countered. "What can I do for you? Is Abigail alright? Is Miriam doing well?"

"Abigail is over there, speaking to Sarah beneath the willow," Jacob said, pointing. He puffed his chest ever so slightly when he said, "Miriam is very well. I will tell her you asked after her. But I have come to see you about a business matter."

"A business matter?" Hannah echoed.

"Concerning your *groossdaadi*. I understand Miriam has shared her condition with you, and I would like your *groossdaadi* to craft a cradle for the *bobbel*, a rocker for Miriam and perhaps a chest of drawers, as well."

"Of course," Hannah agreed, although she was surprised by the request. She wondered if Jacob was being charitable because he knew her income would soon cease. He needn't have made such a gesture—she'd have enough money from watching the Plank children to tide them over until she found another way to make ends meet. "But isn't the cradle my *groossdaadi* made before Abigail was born in *gut* condition still?"

"It is. At least I think it is," Jacob replied, a shadow crossing his brow. "After Miriam lost the second *bobbel*, it was too painful of a reminder to keep around. We gave it to her sister-in-law, and as you know, she and her husband and *kinner* have long since moved to Indiana."

"Of course. I will speak to *Groossdaadi* tonight about making the cradle. I know he'll get started right away," Hannah said, sorry she had pressed Jacob about the old cradle. There was a reason topics like this were rarely mentioned, even between long-standing friends. "He will make it nice and sturdy, to hold your bouncing boy, *Gott* willing."

Miriam had confessed to Hannah that Jacob hoped to be blessed with the birth of a boy, so her remark caused a grin to spread across his face. "*Denki*, Hannah."

After he left, it was Hannah who was thanking the Lord for His provision once again. With her income as a nanny and the project for her grandfather, they'd have enough to see them into the winter. *Surely* Gott *will continue to provide*, she thought, and the tiredness she had experienced moments earlier was quickly replaced with such light-hearted energy it carried her through the day.

On the way home, she led the children through the wooded area bordering the fields. Although the jaunt took longer than usual, she figured it didn't matter if she was later returning home, since she had three more pairs of hands helping with the evening chores. Besides, the trees provided shade from the relentless sun, and the stream was a refreshing resting place. As soon as they arrived, the boys capered from rock to rock.

"Samuel, you're splashing Teacher!" Sarah scolded after the boy lifted a large stone and let it drop again.

"He *is* splashing me," Hannah said. "And it's nice and icy cold. Here, feel—"

She dipped her fingers in the water and flicked them at Sarah, who screwed up her face as if she couldn't believe Hannah would do such a thing.

"Be careful—she will tattle on you to *Daed*," Simon accused. "Sarah always tattles."

"Does she really?" Hannah kidded him. "Because to my ears right now it sounds a bit as if *you* are tattling on *her*." With a wink at Sarah, Hannah cupped her hands, lifted a scoop of water and flung it in Simon's direction, dousing him.

Soon, the four of them had squealed, splashed and laughed the afternoon away. Hannah couldn't remember having such fun since she and her sister were children frolicking there themselves.

Sweat soaked Sawyer's shirt and he briefly considered changing it, but his others were just as dirty. The four men tried to keep up with the laundry and housework, and Sarah participated in chores beyond her years, but with three of the men in the fields all day and John doddering on crutches, certain tasks took less priority than others.

As he headed toward Hannah's house, he consoled himself with the thought that they'd only be there for a short season. He was much more effective at hewing wood than at harvesting fields, and he'd be glad to get back to Ohio and his business. He'd be gladder still for Gertrude's return, so their lives could resume as usual. His young sister was not yet the accomplished cook their mother or Eliza had been, but she was certainly more skilled than his uncle.

As the buggy bounced over a dip in the road, Sawyer's stomach lurched. Whatever else had been in the chicken casserole John had served for dinner, it was making Sawyer queasy now. But as he pulled into the lane where Hannah lived, his nausea was replaced by a burst of cheer at seeing Simon and Sarah each holding a handle of a wheelbarrow as they gave Samuel a ride across the yard. Hannah was settled in a rocking chair on the porch, leafing through *Blackboard Bulletin*, a magazine for teachers.

"Hello, Hannah," he said from a distance, removing his hat as the children bounded across the yard to put away the wheelbarrow and then gather their schoolbooks from inside the house.

"Hello, Sawyer," Hannah replied. "Please, *kumme* sit. The *kinner* will be a few moments."

"I shouldn't." He hesitated. "I'm afraid I smell like I live in a sty."

"Not at all," she countered. "You're fine. Just fine."

There it was again, that lilt in her voice and the repetition of the very phrase he had used earlier that caused him to wonder if she was making light or if he'd seriously offended her with his previous comments about her appearance. In either case, it caught him off guard and he didn't know how to interpret it, so he changed the subject to a blander topic.

"I hear we're in for some more big storms, which should break the heat. It sure feels more like July than September."

"It does," she agreed amicably. "But don't be fooled. The days are definitely getting shorter. It won't be long until it's dark by this time of evening."

"Aw, will we still be able to play outside?" Simon asked from the doorway. "It's my turn in the wheelbarrow tomorrow."

"You shouldn't interrupt adult conversation," Sawyer reprimanded. "But *jah*, there's still plenty of time for each of you to have several turns in the wheelbarrow."

"Gut," said Simon. "Because we don't have a wheelbarrow in Ohio."

Sawyer contradicted him. "Actually, Simon, we have two wheelbarrows."

"But it's not the same. It's funner here," Simon argued.

"Funnier," Sarah corrected him.

"More funny," Samuel chimed in.

"Everything is *more fun* when you're playing in a wheelbarrow instead of working with it," Hannah agreed. "Especially if you're playing with people you like. And if you've had a *gut* night's sleep, which is what you need. So, I will see you tomorrow, *Gott* willing, when it will be Simon's turn in the wheelbarrow."

Even in the dusky light, Hannah's infectious smile caused Sawyer to grin back at her, certain now that nothing he said that morning had caused her any offense. In fact, it was likely the opposite was true, and any lingering embarrassment he felt was replaced by a sense of delight.

"My brother and sister-in-law will be going to visit John Plank on Sunday," Doris told Hannah on Friday morning before school began.

Services were held every other Sunday, and this was an "off Sunday," when most families would hold their own worship time together in the morning and then visit other people in the district in the afternoon.

"Our visit is long overdue. We should have gone round when John was first injured. But better late than never," Doris explained. "Besides, with four men fending for themselves during harvest, I suppose they'd *wilkom* receiving an apple crisp no matter when it arrives."

"That's very hospitable of you," Hannah replied, not rising to the bait.

She suspected Doris was more interested in cozying up to Sawyer than she was in the general welfare of John Plank's household, but she quickly dismissed the thought as judgmental. Besides, she felt a bit peaked from the heat. She ducked off the front steps and into the classroom, leaving Doris alone to usher the children into the building.

By the end of the day, she felt no better and the children seemed to be sagging on the way home, as well. They crossed over the stream without stopping to look under stones or attempting to get each other wet. After the boys finished their chore of picking up stray sticks and pulling weeds from the garden and Sarah had swept the porch and kitchen, Hannah suggested they let the chickens out to roam, which was usually a source of great amusement.

"Can we read instead?" Samuel asked, an uncharacteristic whine in his voice, his eyes a paler shade of green than usual.

Hannah deduced Sarah must have been ailing, too, because she didn't tell Samuel to say *may* instead of *can*.

"Jah," Hannah answered, wiping her hand along the back of her neck. "I will bring you a cool drink. I am hot and thirsty myself."

She had just finished slicing a lemon when she heard a gagging cough she instinctively recognized that meant a child was on the brink of getting sick, and she raced into the parlor and shoved a bin under Samuel's mouth. In rapid succession, Simon and Sarah were sick, as well, and although Hannah felt her stomach constrict, she managed to press on, giving each child a tepid bath, fitting them with nightshirts and tucking them into bed. She put Simon and Samuel in the double bed in Eve's old room, and Sarah into her own double bed. Hannah made several trips between the two rooms, wringing cool compresses and arranging pillows before the children were soothed enough to sleep.

Waves of nausea washed over her as she prepared her grandfather's supper, and a wet V formed on the back of her dress, but she served the meal on time. She could hardly stand the aroma of food, but she took a seat opposite her grandfather to keep him company.

"The *kinner* didn't come today?" he asked loudly as he eyed the empty spots around the table.

"*Jah*, they are here. They got sick," she mouthed. "They're in bed upstairs."

Her grandfather jabbed his fork into a slice of meat and said, "They cannot stay."

Hannah leaned toward him so he would know she was speaking. "*Neh*, they cannot *leave*. They are ill."

The force of her own determination surprised her. Her entire life, Hannah had never spoken back to her grandfather and she wouldn't have contradicted him now if the children weren't sick, but their vulnerable condition ignited a maternal protectiveness she didn't know she possessed. Whether she was running a fever or it was from the strength of her convictions, her face felt fiery and she began to shake so noticeably that she rose, turning her back on her grandfather to rinse the dirty pans until her hands were steady again. By that time, he had vacated the room.

* * *

As soon as Hannah opened the door, Sawyer knew something was wrong.

"The *kinner* are fine," she immediately told him, quelling the pounding in his ears. "But they had upset stomachs. I have put them to bed."

"But they are all okay?" Sawyer asked.

"Nothing a *gut* night's sleep won't cure," Hannah assured him. "Some of the other scholars have had this, too. It's a twenty-four-hour flu."

"I am sorry for any inconven—"

"You needn't apologize. I'm relieved they're resting. Since they'd be coming back tomorrow anyway, I think it best they spend the night here. It will save you another trip in the morning."

"I couldn't allow you to do that," Sawyer protested.

"You couldn't *stop* me from doing that," Hannah quipped, her hands on her hips. "The *kinner* need uninterrupted sleep. It's no trouble for me, and no amount of noise would ever wake *Groossdaadi*."

Sawyer could plainly see Hannah looked a bit frayed around the edges herself, although he wasn't about to make the same mistake by mentioning to her how tired she appeared. *"Denki,"* he said, gazing into her eyes. "Would it be alright if I looked in on them before I leave?"

"Of course."

Hannah tiptoed up the stairs and Sawyer followed, trying to keep his boots from clunking through the hall. The boys were lying back-to-back, breathing in unison, even in sleep.

"*Gute nacht*, Samuel. *Gute nacht*, Simon," Sawyer bade them.

Pushing open the door to her room, Hannah whispered, "Sarah will share her bed with me."

Sawyer peered in at his daughter, who had curled herself around a pillow. "You're aware she sometimes wakes screaming from nightmares."

"If she does, I will comfort her," Hannah promised.

"Of that, I have no doubt," Sawyer replied. "I mention it more for your sake than hers. I'd hate to have her startle you. As the saying goes, it can be a rude awakening."

"I'll be fine," Hannah insisted. "We both will be."

Before dropping off to sleep later that night, Sawyer found himself wondering who comforted Hannah when she was ill. Certainly not that grandfather of hers. Even if he were inclined to help, he couldn't hear her request for a drink of water or a cool compress.

He recalled the many times he had sat on the edge of the bed when Eliza was sick, wishing there was something else he could do to help her.

"Your prayers are most helpful," she would say. "And your presence is a kind of balm. How terrible it would feel to be sick and all alone."

Remembering, Sawyer prayed, *Dear Lord,* denki *for providing someone as competent and kind as Hannah to watch the* kinner, *so I can sleep well knowing they are under her care. Please heal them and keep Hannah from becoming ill herself. And please give them all a sense of Your loving presence, just as You've given me. Amen.*

Chapter Six

It was Samuel, not Sarah, who woke Hannah in the middle of the night. She rushed to his side with a bin and towel, but he wasn't ill; he was merely confused about where he was. The commotion woke Simon, as well.

"I will sit here on the end of the bed until you both fall asleep again," she offered.

"Will you tell us a story?" Samuel asked. "*Daed* sometimes tells us stories."

"What kind of stories does your *daed* tell?"

"Stories about our *mamm*," mumbled Simon. "About how she swept his feet off."

Hannah scrunched her brow. "Swept him off his feet?"

"Jah." Samuel yawned. "Because she had a kind heart."

"Such a kind heart that the Lord blessed her with three *bobblin* at once so her kindness wouldn't go to waste," Simon added. "*Waste not, want not*, our *mamm* always said."

"That sounds like a *wunderbaar* story," Hannah replied. "What else happens in that tale?"

But the boys had already fallen back asleep, so she slipped out of the room, leaving the door ajar a crack. Sarah was sprawled across the center of the bed, so Hannah stretched sideways along the outer edge, careful not to rouse her. Her limbs ached, and as she tried to fall asleep, she thought about Sawyer bidding his children good-night and about the bedtime story the boys indicated he shared with them. How had she ever made the mistake of thinking Sawyer was too forbidding? She had never known a man to be so tender to his children, and she assumed he must have been equally affectionate to his wife. She nodded off, wistfully imagining what it would be like to have a husband like that.

For breakfast, she served the children broth and toast in bed, and by ten thirty, the boys were roughhousing—bouncing on the bed and smacking each other with pillows.

"If you're well enough to wrestle, you're well enough to clean the coop," she said, shooing them outdoors.

Sarah slept in, but by noon she joined her brothers romping on the lawn. Hannah, however, weakened as the day wore on. She held her nose as she fixed supper and excused herself from the room while the others ate. When she heard Sawyer's buggy, she mustered the last of her strength to send the children off before collapsing into bed.

Sawyer was pleased with what he and his cousins had accomplished that Saturday on the farm, but as he guided the horse away from Hannah's home, he worried that their progress had come at too great a cost to Hannah, even if the children were no worse for the wear.

"Hannah served us our breakfast in bed!" the boys reported.

"She helped me write a letter to Gertrude," Sarah informed him.

Sawyer wondered how Hannah had managed, given how sick she looked. Despite his prayers for the contrary, her eyes were a watery blue and her skin sallow. Even her smile appeared feeble. Rationally, he expected Hannah would be fine, but his experience of watching Eliza's condition deteriorate so quickly had made him hypervigilant. He'd learned not to take his loved ones' health for granted.

He reminded himself that Hannah wasn't his loved one, of course. But he did care about her health, and before shutting his eyes for the evening, he prayed again. *Lord, please give Hannah rest today and tomorrow, so she will be well again. Not just for the* kinner's *sake, but for her own.*

The next morning the four men and three children spent quiet time together in Scripture reading and prayer, as was the custom every other Sunday when they didn't meet for church. They sang hymns, and after eating a simple noon meal, the children were allowed to go outside to play quietly. Ordinarily, Sawyer might have enjoyed strolling with them through the meadows, but after their illness, he wanted to subdue their activity, so he remained on the porch, watching as they combed the lawn for grasshoppers.

The week's farmwork had done him in: his eyelids grew heavy, and he leaned his head back against the railing. The next thing he knew, a buggy was pulling up the lane carrying Doris Hooley, her sister-in-law, Amelia, and her brother, James, whom Sawyer had met last Sunday.

"Guder nammidaag," he greeted them.

"Guder nammidaag," Doris sang, holding out a large rectangular glass dish. "We brought apple crisp for you."

"For everyone." Amelia quickly made the distinction. "We hope we caught you in time for tea."

"I'm not sure John has teacups," Sawyer replied with a chuckle. "But we can put on a pot of coffee. Don't let my cousins see that crisp or it'll be gone before you have a chance to sit down."

He had noticed that despite their superficial disdain for treats, his cousins never passed up any dessert his uncle purchased in town. But it was Samuel, not his cousins, who spied the treat first.

"Apple crisp!" he exclaimed.

"I'm sorry, but none for you," Sawyer said, eliciting

cries of disappointment from all three of the children. He turned to Doris to explain. "They were sick last night, I'm afraid."

"That's a shame," Doris said, clucking her tongue. Then she added brightly, "The more for us!"

Sawyer refrained from shaking his head. The woman was candid to a fault about what she wanted.

As the adults gathered for refreshments, Sawyer's uncle apologized for the general state of the house. Amelia politely denied noticing any disarray, but Doris looked around the room and sniffed before saying, "A house needs a woman's touch to make it a home. It can't be easy looking after the *kinner*, harvesting and keeping house."

"Hannah Lantz cares for the *kinner* after school," Sawyer quickly emphasized. He didn't want Doris volunteering her services again. "But when they're here, they participate in chores the best they can."

"She's right," John interjected. "We could use help with mending and laundering. Perhaps a hot meal. I do my best, but it's difficult working one-handed, balancing on a crutch like I have to."

"Of course it is," cooed Doris. "Say no more. It would be a privilege to help a neighbor in need."

Sawyer went silent; it wasn't his home, so it wasn't his place to comment. When the guests were leaving and the crisp was only three-fourths gone, Doris suggested Sawyer save it for the children's lunch the next day.

"What about your dish?" he asked thoughtfully. "Won't you need it for baking?"

"Oh, I'll be visiting a lot more often, so I'll pick it up the next time I'm here," she said, before flouncing to the buggy.

Hannah spent the better portion of Sunday in bed, rising only for Scripture reading and worship with her grandfather and to fix his meals. By evening she felt well enough to pen a letter to her sister.

My dearest Eve,

What a joy to hear about the Lord's blessings to you and Menno! I will pray for all to go well. I relish the thought of holding a baby in my arms, and I know you relish it even more.

I was also pleased to hear Menno's repair shop is flourishing and it isn't necessary for you to make quilts for consignment anymore. It's very generous of you to offer to continue quilting in order to send the income to Grandfather and me, but the Lord has provided for us in another way.

As you recall from my earlier letters, John Plank broke his leg in a ditch. He and his sons couldn't manage harvest season on their own, so recently, his nephew, Sawyer Plank, arrived to help. Sawyer is a cabinetmaker from Ohio who has triplets, Simon, Sarah and Samuel, seven years of age. Although Sawyer is widowed, he has not remarried. I have been hired to bring his children home with me in the afternoon and prepare their supper here. Afterward, Sawyer picks them up. He has been most generous with my salary, and this short-term arrangement should provide Grandfather and me our daily bread until I find other work.

The children are a delight to care for, and they're a big help to me with evening chores. I am teaching Sarah baking basics. Simon and Samuel are so active that sometimes I think I am seeing quadruple instead of just double when they scamper about the yard! Samuel is the tiniest bit stronger and quicker than

Simon, but Simon makes up for it by trying twice as hard. Sarah keeps her brothers in line by "correcting" their grammar and scolding them for perceived offenses, although they are never truly naughty. We laugh much of the time we are together and I am sorry to see them leave in the evening.

Sawyer Plank is a very tall man with a solemn face, pensive green eyes and a voice deeper than Grandfather's. Yet despite his size, he is exceptionally gentle with his children and there are times when a laugh breaks through his seriousness, making his eyes dance. He sometimes stammers and is more often than not reserved in nature, but I understand now this is because he is thoughtful, not arrogant. Anyone who doesn't hold a grudge against another for nearly running over his foot with their buggy—as Grandfather nearly did in town the other day—must have a forbearing spirit. Sawyer has certainly been thoughtful in supplementing our pantry, as well, and I appreciate how considerate he is of our situation.

Grandfather's health is well (even if his steering is not!). Our apples are early and copious this year, and I will try the recipe you sent as a special treat for my scholars before I bid them goodbye. As fond as she is of desserts, Doris Hooley does not allow such celebrations in her classroom.

Grandfather and I would like to visit you soon, God willing.

Please remember me to Menno and write again with news of how you are.

Your loving sister,
Hannah

* * *

After Doris, Amelia and James left on Sunday afternoon, Sawyer provided the children with sheets of paper for drawing while he wrote letters.

The first was to the foreman of the shop. *Has Vernon's hand healed enough to carry out his daily work?* he inquired.

Then he directed:

> If not, assign your duties to him—managing orders, the books and scheduling deliveries to the English; everything except overseeing the rest of the crew. You alone are responsible for their charge, along with performing any work Vernon would do, had he not been injured.

When he had finished addressing matters of business to his foreman, he began a letter to his sister.

> Dear Gertrude,
>
> I am thankful Kathryn and the baby are gaining strength. We will continue to ask the Lord's will for them. Remember us to Kathryn and Leroy. John and your cousins also send their greetings.
>
> Sarah's nightmares have decreased, although she still misses you. Samuel and Simon say they especially miss your mashed potato candy on Sunday evenings. The children are faring well in school: Sarah is writing you a letter, as she has mastered the spelling and printing of many small words.
>
> Their schoolteacher is Hannah Lantz and I have hired her to care for them through the supper hour as well as give them their nighttime baths, and she

even manages to untangle Sarah's hair without a fuss. Although Hannah is petite in form, she matches the children's vibrancy. They amuse me with stories of their daily escapades together all the way home after I pick them up from her grandfather's house, where she lives. (It is strange she is unmarried, but Willow Creek is a small town and perhaps her suitable choices were few.) She is a fine teacher, too. I concentrate on the farmwork better, knowing her deep blue eyes are keeping careful watch over the children.

The harvesting is as to be expected. We are working as diligently as possible. I am grateful for the strength the Lord provides me in order to help John during this time of need.

I was informed Vernon Mast was injured. I don't know how they are keeping up in the shop, with two fewer men (Vernon and myself) to share the load. God willing, Vernon will be healed and I will make headway here so I can return sooner rather than later.

Your brother,
Sawyer

PS: I miss your Sunday-evening mashed potato candy as much as the boys do, but don't tell your uncle I said that. He's doing the best he can.

"Sawyer mentioned the *kinner* were sick," Doris said on Monday morning. She stood over Hannah's desk eating a doughnut.

"Sawyer is here? I didn't see him arrive with the *kinner* yet."

Doris licked powdered sugar from her fingers. "*Neh*, he's not here. He told me yesterday, when we visited John Plank. They seemed alright to me, though. You have to be careful with *kinner*—they'll feign illness to be excused from their chores."

"I'm wise to the ways of *kinner*, and they were genuinely sick," Hannah snapped. "Not to mention, they had already finished their chores when they became ill."

Doris shrugged. "They seemed fine when I saw them, so I didn't want anyone taking advantage of you. You look a little under the weather yourself."

"I am fine, *denki*," Hannah replied in a milder voice.

The inactivity on Sunday had been helpful; she was all but recovered, although the sight of Doris chewing a doughnut still put her stomach on edge.

"It's time to summon the *kinner* for class," she suggested.

Just as Doris and Hannah exited the building, Sawyer was taking the stairs by twos, a glass dish in his hand.

"*Guder mariye*, Hannah," he exclaimed breathlessly.

"*Guder mariye*, Sawyer," Doris interrupted pointedly before Hannah could answer.

"Forgive my manners," Sawyer mumbled, looking chagrined. "*Guder mariye*, Doris. I've brought your dish."

"I told you I would have retrieved that when I visit the farm tomorrow." Doris pouted.

"I wanted to save you the trouble."

"It's no trouble—I'll be going there anyway," Doris replied. To Hannah she expounded, "I'll be helping with some of the household chores on the farm. Of course, I wouldn't accept a penny for it. I consider it my Christian duty to help a neighbor in need."

Hannah felt her cheeks flame. Whether it was embarrassment because she needed to accept compensation for helping Sawyer's family or the glare of the morning sun, she didn't know, but suddenly she couldn't get out of Doris and Sawyer's presence quickly enough.

"That's very kind of you," she said to Doris, and then she spun on her heel toward the classroom.

The sudden movement caused her such wooziness, she teetered backward. In the split second it took her to become aware she was going to tumble backward down the stairs, she felt Sawyer's strong hands clasp her shoulders, propping her upright.

"Easy does it," he said into her ear, sliding his hands down to clutch her elbows.

Stunned and dizzy, she was in no condition to resist when he steered her inside and settled her into her chair. Using what Sarah referred to as his "big voice," he ordered Doris to bring her a glass of water.

"I'm fine, really," she insisted while the two of them watched her sip the water until it was gone. "It was the heat."

"Then why are you still quivering?" Sawyer asked.

He crouched by her side so he could be level with her face. He gazed so intently into her eyes, she nearly confessed it was the unfamiliar warmth of a man's touch that had unnerved her so.

Instead, she blinked and said, "I'm faint because I haven't been eating enough, perhaps."

"You caught what the *kinner* had, didn't you?" Sawyer asked accusingly. "I don't think you should be here at school today."

Hannah drew herself up to her full height. "Don't be ridiculous," she objected adamantly. "I'm fine. Listen—the scholars are arriving. *Denki* for your concern, but lessons are about to begin. I'll walk you to the door."

* * *

Sawyer hung back before following her outside. He knew not to argue with a woman who had made up her mind as definitively as Hannah had. But all the way back to the farm and throughout the day, he thought about her frail form in his arms. She had looked as pale as a sheet.

Finally, he decided that she may have made up her mind, but so had he. When class was letting out, he hitched up the horse and clopped to the schoolhouse. Everyone else was gone, and he knew he could find Sarah, Simon and Samuel inside helping Hannah wash the blackboards.

"Hello, *kinner*," he said. "Hello, Hannah."

"Hello, *Daed*," they chorused as Hannah quickly made her way to his side.

"Is something wrong?" she whispered, her brow knitted.

"Not at all," he faltered, suddenly feeling foolish. "I have an errand to run in town. I thought I'd bring you all home on the way."

"That's very thoughtful," Hannah said skeptically, "but we're in the opposite direction from town. You will have to backtrack."

Sawyer shrugged. "It's no bother."

Hannah tipped her head as if about to expose his falsehood with a joke, but then she seemed to change her mind. "*Kumme*, let's not keep your *daed* waiting," she said to the children.

At the buggy, he took Hannah's graceful fingers in one of his hands and supported her elbow with the other, easing her into the front seat.

"You are being too kind." She laughed breezily.

The sensation of her satiny skin against his caused the tiny hairs along his arms to stand on end. His head spun and his stomach somersaulted so fiercely he wondered if he was coming down with something himself. Yet as he sat beside Hannah, who engaged the children with amusing anecdotes all the way home, he felt anything but sick. Indeed, he felt better than he had in a long, long time.

"I can't eat this." Hannah's grandfather threw the crust onto his plate. "It's tough."

Sarah looked as if she'd been slapped. She had been so pleased Hannah allowed her to help, but in her enthusiasm she'd added too much flour to the bread dough.

You are the one who is tough, Hannah thought.

She held her glass in front of her mouth so her grandfather wouldn't see her lips moving.

"You mustn't pay him any mind, Sarah. He hasn't got all his teeth, so it's difficult for him to chew. This is a fine first effort. If we don't eat it all, I can use what's left for bread crumbs in a stuffing."

"It tastes *gut* if you soak it in your gravy," Samuel said, a kindness that made Hannah want to hug him.

Simon added, "Or dip it in your milk."

Sarah nodded bravely, her eyes brimming.

Hannah remembered all too well how many times her grandfather's cutting words reduced her to near tears when she was a child. She thought she was past being hurt by his criticism, but that evening, after Sawyer and the children left, he approached her in the parlor, where she was patching a tear in his pants.

"I saw him bring you home," he said.

She was so surprised by her grandfather's statement, at first she didn't know what he was talking about. She searched his face for a clue.

"Sawyer Plank," her grandfather explained.

"*Jah*, he said he was running an errand in town," she

mouthed. "But I suspect since we had been ill, he wanted to spare us walking in the heat."

Her grandfather jabbed a finger in the air in Hannah's direction. "You are too old to be acting like a schoolgirl being courted home from a singing. Especially with your employer."

He shuffled off to his bedroom without waiting for a reply.

Hannah's eyes momentarily welled, but her hurt was quickly replaced by a sense of fury. As weak as she'd felt that morning, her grandfather's remark sparked a new vigor, and she pricked her fingers so many times she finally tossed her mending aside. She didn't know what offended her more: that her grandfather demonstrated so little appreciation for the fact she was doing her best to earn extra income, which obligated them to maintain friendly rapport with Sawyer, or that her grandfather would begrudge her a ride home after she'd been ill.

However, by the time she'd finished slamming through her evening chores, she was physically and emotionally spent. She sat on the sofa and picked up her grandfather's pants to finish stitching the patch. As she sewed, she realized how threadbare the fabric had become. It made her think of the many sacrifices her grandfather must have made in order to raise her and her sister.

Besides the Lord, who had ever supported her and cared for her for as many years and in as many ways as her family? The nanny opportunity was a blessing, but it was temporary. Soon Sawyer and the children would return to Ohio. As fond as she was of the Plank family, her relationship with them was a way to earn money. Her life was in Willow Creek, where her grandfather was—she was sure that was all he meant to remind her of with his cutting tone.

It was past eleven o'clock when she finally closed the

door to her bedroom and knelt beside her bed. *Lord,* she prayed, *please forgive my anger. Thank You for providing for me through* Groossdaadi *all of these years. Please bless him with a* gut *night's sleep and help Sarah, Simon and Samuel to get the rest they need, as well.*

But it was Sawyer who filled her mind's eye as she lay sleepless in the dark. As humid as the air was, when she recalled his arms bracing her when she stumbled on the steps or his masculine grip as he aided her into the buggy, a shiver ran down her spine. He had treated her as if she was even more precious cargo than her grandfather's dollhouse!

The thought made her feel as giddy as a schoolgirl—and then she remembered her grandfather's words: "You are too old to be acting like a schoolgirl being courted home from a singing. Especially with your employer." She feared her grandfather had hit the nail on the head: instead of behaving like "every bit the woman" Sawyer believed she was, she had been acting like a teenager with a crush, swooning and giggling over his smallest friendly gesture.

She reminded herself that such feelings were fleeting—and soon Sawyer would be fleeting, too. Meanwhile, what would he think if he knew she felt this way? Even from a distance, her grandfather had noticed her juvenile levity. What if Sawyer had, too? Would he think she was too irresponsible and immature to oversee his children? Would he dismiss her as a "desperate Doris"?

She could neither risk losing her nanny job nor could she stand the comparison, so before closing her eyes a final time for sleep, she resolved to behave more appropriately in the future.

Exhausted as he was, Sawyer tossed and turned, wondering if Hannah knew how holding her that morning had affected him. Had she felt his hands tremble? Did she think he was terribly presumptuous showing up to usher her home after school and again taking her by the arm? He hadn't been able to help himself. She seemed so delicate, and no matter how vehemently she objected, Sawyer didn't think she ought to walk in the sweltering weather.

Even toward the end of her illness, Eliza used to claim she felt better than her health implied. Sawyer remembered one time when she patted the bed, gesturing for him to sit with her. Her voice was raspy and her breathing labored. He tried to hush her, but she said it was very important that he listen to what she had to say.

"After I am gone," she began, "there is something I want you to do for me."

Sawyer stood up. "I'll have none of that—" he protested, but she clasped his hand and pulled him back into a sitting position.

"Sawyer, my dear, you must listen and do what I ask," she pleaded. "First, remember me to the *kinner* always."

Sawyer nodded. "I will," he promised. His eyes grew moist, but he couldn't let his wife see how her words pained him.

"I want you to remarry—"

"Neh!" he exclaimed, jumping up and pacing to the window, his back toward her. "Never."

His wife did something then that surprised him—she laughed. From her sickbed, she laughed.

He spun on his heel. "Is this a joke?" he fumed.

"Neh, neh," she softly shushed him. "I couldn't be more serious about anything in my life. It's just that you sounded like Samuel the day we told him he'd eventually grow up and love a girl and get married and move away from us."

Sawyer stood where he was, tears streaming down his face as he stared out the window.

"Sawyer," Eliza continued. "The *kinner* need a *mamm*."

"*You're* their *mamm*," he argued belligerently.

She continued as if she hadn't heard. "And you need a wife to love you."

"Your love is enough to last a lifetime," he heard himself say.

Eliza coughed several times, and Sawyer returned to the bed to kneel by her side. When she had caught her breath again, she stroked his hair.

"You have so much love to give," she whispered. "You need to give it to a wife." Then, teasing, she added, "Waste not, want not."

"There will never be another like you, Eliza," he cried, burying his head in her shoulder.

"*Neh*, but there *will be* another," she said firmly. "When you find her, you have my blessing, because I know the woman you choose—and the woman the Lord provides for you—will be worthy of your love."

Remembering, Sawyer kicked at his sheets and shifted to his side. He hardly knew Hannah. How preposterous it was to think he might feel a stirring of emotion for her as a woman. Yes, she took good care of the children, but so would anyone he hired in Ohio. And Ohio was where his home was, where his livelihood was and where he was meant to be. This life in Pennsylvania was temporary, and so was the brief kindling of connection he felt with Hannah. It couldn't hold a candle to the steadfast love he'd shared with Eliza during their six-year marriage.

I'm acting like a charmed schoolboy, he thought. He decided he must take care not to confuse his appreciation for Hannah as a hired nanny with any other emotion. From now on, he'd be more mindful that their relationship was built on business and more careful to keep his distance.

Chapter Seven

Hannah's decision to behave in a manner more becoming of a mature schoolteacher and nanny when she was around Sawyer proved easier to practice than she expected. Tuesday through Thursday, Sawyer dropped the children off at school and picked them up with nary a word about anything other than the weather, which remained uncomfortably humid.

On Friday morning, it was Doris who greeted Sawyer at the base of the stairs, so when Hannah saw him there, she returned to her classroom. She figured if Doris wanted to sidle up to him with another apple crisp, she could give it her best effort. He'd probably grumble later that it sat in his stomach like a brick anyway.

She immediately scolded herself for having such stingy thoughts. She had been uncharacteristically peevish for most of the week, and she couldn't put a finger on what was bothering her. She only knew that once the children left for the evening, she hastily finished her chores and retreated to her room to prepare lessons for the following day. She reasoned there was no sense remaining in the parlor; it wasn't as if her grandfather ever initiated a conversation, and he hardly appeared interested in the topics she brought to his attention.

But her cranky mood always vanished when she was with the children, whose wholesome inquisitiveness and entertaining chatter as they walked home from school buoyed her spirit.

"Can we show *Daed* the stream tonight?" Samuel asked for the second time that week.

"*May* we show *Daed* the stream tonight?" Sarah corrected him in her best teacher voice.

"Please?" Simon added.

Hannah hesitated. Over the past few days she had begun to suspect Sawyer was avoiding her as much as she was avoiding him.

"Your *daed* has seen many streams before," she said.

"*Jah*, but this is a special stream," Samuel said.

"What makes it special?"

"It's *your* stream," he said.

Hannah was tickled by the sentiment, but said, "I think after a difficult day of working in the fields, your *daed's* feet are sore and he doesn't want to walk all the way to the stream."

"But that is exactly why we must take him there," Simon contended. "He can take off his shoes and socks and soak his sore feet in the water. It always makes *my* toes feel better."

Hannah chuckled at Simon's logic. "*Jah*, I know it does, Simon. I have to mention to your *daed* that your shoes are pinching your toes. I think you're going through a growth spurt. It's permissible for you to go barefoot now, but later in the fall, you'll need proper-fitting shoes."

"But can we show him the stream?"

"*Jah*, you may," she replied.

If it meant that much to the children, she didn't see harm in allowing them to take their father to the stream. Besides, they knew the way there; it wasn't as if she had to accompany them. She would wait to see how Sawyer reacted to the suggestion. She hoped by that evening any awkwardness between them would have passed and Sawyer would know how sensible she was, despite her temporary lapse in appropriate behavior.

But that evening, it was John Plank and Doris, not Sawyer, who arrived to gather the children.

Hannah was so surprised, she rushed across the grass to the buggy and blurted out, "Where is Sawyer? Is he alright?"

"What a nervous Nellie you are," scoffed Doris. "He's fine."

"The boys had work left to accomplish," explained John. "There may be bad weather tomorrow, so they wanted to finish as much as they could tonight."

Doris boasted, "After I surprised them when I dropped in to cook a hearty meal, they had the strength to complete their work. John and I thought since my horse was already out, we'd use my buggy to pick up the triplets. Besides, as you can guess, John can't get into and out of the buggy without an adult to help him."

Hannah marveled that there was no end to what Doris would do to catch a man's attention. But she doubted her efforts would amount to anything anyway; Sawyer didn't appear interested in her.

After the triplets had been rounded up and the buggy was ready to depart, John snapped his fingers and said, "I almost forgot. Sawyer had a message for you."

Anticipation fluttered in Hannah's chest. *"Jah?"*

"He said if it is raining tomorrow, please don't expect Sarah, Simon and Samuel," John stated. "Although he said, of course, you'd be compensated for the full week, regardless of the weather."

Hannah's cheeks burned. Sawyer's offer further emphasized that their connection was based solely on an employment relationship, and she found it insulting he'd suggest she expected payment for a service she didn't provide.

"Please tell Sawyer I said he might better spend his money on new shoes for the boys—their feet have outgrown the pairs they have now."

She strode toward the house without another word.

Sawyer swatted at a fly buzzing around his ear as he pitched hay in the horses' stalls. He felt as ornery as a mule. Admittedly the yumasetta casserole Doris made was delicious, but he would have preferred eating one of his uncle's unsavory concoctions in silence to listening to Doris prattling at dinner. Furthermore, because of Doris's insistence that she and John pick up the children, Sawyer missed seeing Hannah that evening. If it rained, he wouldn't see her on Saturday, either.

He noticed she'd been out of sorts all week, and he was concerned he had offended her by his behavior on Monday. Or was it an issue of money—perhaps taking care of the children was worth more than he was paying her, especially when they were sick? Did she regret taking on the position after all? At least if it rained tomorrow, she'd have a day to herself. Perhaps that was what she desired.

He resolved to speak to her candidly about it on Saturday if it didn't rain, or on Sunday if it did. Church was scheduled to meet at James and Amelia Hooley's house this Sabbath. The only obstacle Sawyer could foresee was that Doris was sure to be around, since she lived with them, but he was determined to somehow seek Hannah out alone.

Much to Sawyer's relief, by the time he returned to the house, Doris was gone.

"Are the *kinner* in bed?" he asked his uncle.

"Doris said they were asleep before their heads hit the

pillow. Hannah Lantz must keep them busy and well fed. They are sleeping better, *jah*?"

"Jah," Sawyer affirmed, grinning. "She is doing them *gut*."

"She is doing you all *gut*," his uncle replied. "Doris was right—a house needs a woman's touch to make it a home."

Sawyer wondered what he was getting at. He shrugged and said, "*Jah*, I am glad I hired her."

"Speaking of that," John said, "Hannah rejected your offer of being compensated if it rains tomorrow and Samuel, Sarah and Simon stay here on the farm. She said your money is better spent on new shoes for the *kinner*."

"She said *what*?" Sawyer asked. "What were her exact words?"

John snorted. "I didn't write them down, man! I only recall that she bristled a bit at the mention of her salary."

Sawyer was flummoxed. Even when he didn't speak with Hannah in person, he managed to bungle his words. He'd have to set it right first thing in the morning.

But when he awoke on Saturday, a heavy rain was thrumming against the roof, thwarting his plans and making for another agonizingly long day without talking to Hannah.

The driving rain did nothing to cool the temperature; instead, the air felt tropical and oppressive. Hannah had just completed her housework when her grandfather asked her to accompany him to town. Although it was pouring, the sky was white, not dark. Hannah figured it wouldn't produce the kind of severe storm that made both her and the horse nervous, so she agreed to go.

Indeed, by the time they arrived in town, the rain had subsided enough for Hannah to dash into the mercantile without getting drenched, while her grandfather visited the hardware store. Once home, she prepared and served dinner and then cleaned and put away the dishes. Afterward, she felt so listless, she baked a triple batch of molasses cookies to bring to James and Amelia's home for church. Usually the family hosting church on a particular week provided the midday meal, but they wouldn't turn away dessert, so Hannah baked enough to feed the entire district.

"Smells *gut*," her grandfather huffed when he entered the kitchen.

She knew from a lifetime of experience that this was his peace offering—a kind word in exchange for a rash of harsh ones. She didn't harbor any bitterness toward him because, as he stood before her, his hands behind his back, she saw him for who he was: a man too stubborn to change, but in need of love just as he was.

"Denki." She smiled. "I have set some cookies aside for you to have with your coffee."

"Here," he said, placing something on the table. "For the girl and her brothers."

It took a moment for Hannah to register what she'd been given: a wooden board, sanded smooth, with two lengths of rope knotted through each end. She realized this was the reason he insisted on going to town today: he needed rope to make a tree swing.

"The *kinner* will enjoy this very much. *Denki, Groossdaadi.*"

Her grandfather grunted and accepted the cup of coffee and plate of cookies she extended to him.

"Their *daed* will have to hang it for them," he said before heading to the parlor. Lest she forget, he reminded her, "And he will need to take it down before they leave. It is only temporary."

Sawyer was relieved when the Sabbath came. His cousins became easily frustrated around the children, and they were especially exasperated when they were cooped up for hours together in the house. He himself felt more and more irascible as the day wore on, the rain a steady deluge against the windows.

"There's no sense in all of us squeezing into one buggy," he announced on Sunday morning. "Besides, my horse needs to stretch its legs."

He left early with the children, intending to speak to Hannah before the services began. He hoped she would be willing to keep an eye on Sarah, Simon and Samuel, since the men sat separately from the women and young children during the services.

But no sooner had he hitched his horse and crossed the yard than Doris appeared out of nowhere.

"*Guder mariye*, Sawyer," she greeted him. "Won't your *onkel* and cousins be coming this morning?"

"Guder mariye," he repeated. "*Jah*, they'll be here soon. We traveled separately."

Sawyer surreptitiously scanned the yard as he was talking to Doris and spotted Hannah far across the lawn.

But before Hannah neared, Doris suggested, "I will watch the *kinner*, so you may go join the other men. They're over there."

Sawyer understood it was customary in this district for the men to gather outside in small groups, usually around the barn, before the services began. Likewise, the women congregated in the kitchen and parlor. At the appropriate time and according to a designated order, the men and women would file into the hosts' meeting room—the Hooleys' basement, in this instance—to worship together. As Jacob Stolzfus signaled to him, Sawyer reluctantly accepted Doris's offer and tramped toward the barn.

A few minutes later, Sawyer took a place on a bench toward the back of the men's section. He hoped Hannah wouldn't think sending the children with Doris was his preference. In fact, he hoped no one thought that, or he'd be the talk of the district.

Yet following lunch, he found out that was exactly what people did think. When he joined a circle of men cavorting in the yard, Jacob commented, "We saw you chatting with Doris this morning and noticed your *kinner* with her, as well. What is the meaning of that?"

"There is no meaning," he stammered. "She offered to oversee the *kinner* during the service and I accepted."

"Are you quite certain about that?"

"Of course I am certain."

"But we have heard her say she has come round to the farm several times recently, supposedly on the pretense of helping with household chores," Jacob pressed. "She's an unmarried woman and you're a widower…yet you still deny she has any designs on you or that you have any interest in courting her?"

In a resounding voice, Sawyer countered, "How many times do I have to tell you, I have no romantic intentions toward that woman? If you must know, I think she behaves more like a silly schoolgirl than a schoolteacher. She is helping my family during a time of need, that is all," he said loudly. "Now if you'll excuse me, I must call my *kinner*."

"There's no need to call them—they are all right here behind you. I brought them over so I could say hello before I left. So, hello, Sawyer. Hello, gentlemen," Hannah said pointedly, acknowledging the small group of men, who suddenly kicked at the dirt or surveyed the clouds. Then, "I will see you tomorrow, Simon, Sarah and Samuel, *Gott* willing."

She had never felt so humiliated in her life, and she

couldn't get away from Sawyer quickly enough. His opinion of her was shameful on its own, but did he have to share it with the other men in her district?

"Hannah, please wait!" he shouted to her, but she pretended to be as deaf as her grandfather as she marched toward the buggy where he was waiting for her.

She was relieved when her grandfather worked the horse into a brisk pace. Back at home, he wandered to his room for a nap and she to the porch to wallow in a good hard cry. She was blowing her nose when a buggy she recognized came up the lane. It was too late to dash inside: Sawyer had already seen her.

"*Guder nammidaag*, Hannah," he called with a friendly wave, as if he hadn't just insulted her and belittled her reputation in front of a half dozen other men.

"Sawyer," she said flatly, glancing beyond him toward the buggy. The children didn't appear to be in it. "Where are Sarah, Simon and Samuel?"

"I left them with my *onkel*," he replied, removing his hat. "Doris said she would see to it he didn't forget to bring them home when he was ready to leave," he joked, but she wouldn't let him wrest a smile from her lips.

He shifted his weight and continued feebly, "Let's just hope she doesn't try to comb Sarah's hair again. Sarah complained she didn't do it as carefully as you do—she said it hurt her scalp—and it doesn't appear as neat, either."

"I'm sure Doris was trying her best." Hannah's temper flared as she rose from her chair. If Sawyer thought insulting Doris was going to distract her from how he insulted her, he was gravely mistaken.

"Of course," Sawyer responded. "It goes without saying Doris did a much better job than I've ever done. I didn't mean to sound ungrateful."

"Just as you didn't mean to sound ungrateful when you

said what you said to Jacob Stolzfus and the others after church? *That* certainly sounded ungrateful to me. And mean-spirited, as well."

Sawyer's mouth stretched into a grim line. "I'm sorry. You are right. I said things I shouldn't have."

"Why are you sorry, Sawyer?" Hannah asked, placing her hands on her hips and glaring down at him on the bottom porch stair. "Is it because your words were untrue? Or is it because they were unkind?"

Sawyer kicked a pebble. "They most definitely were unkind. As for being untrue or not… I am sorry, Hannah, but I cannot be dishonest. I do find Doris's behavior silly at times. My own sister Gertrude is half as young but acts twice as wise."

"Doris?" Hannah gulped. Her knees felt as if they would buckle behind her.

"I know she is a friend of yours, and because of that, I don't doubt she has redeeming qualities," he answered, leaping up the stairs to stand in front of her. "But I have only experienced her superficial side. The other men were pressuring me to claim my intentions toward her, of which I have none. Still, I was wrong to say what I said. Please forgive me for speaking out of turn."

As the realization of her mistake washed over Hannah, she struggled to gain her composure. She was so relieved she didn't accuse Sawyer of what she thought him guilty of saying about her—he would have thought her ten times more nonsensical than Doris.

"I understand," she said slowly. "Although I am not certain the situation warrants it after all, I accept your apology. Especially since you came all this way to express you intended no harm."

* * *

Sawyer took a step backward and leaned against the railing.

"Actually," he admitted, avoiding her radiant blue eyes, "I came because I was afraid I caused you an earlier offense."

"What offense was that?" she asked, her lips pursed.

Sawyer didn't know how he could answer her question without drawing attention to his behavior. If he hadn't offended her in the first place, he didn't want to point it out now.

Stuttering, he replied, "It's just…I, er… I worry I may have been too intrusive. Taking liberties when I shouldn't have."

"I don't know what you mean," she replied. "But I assure you it isn't the case. I am always happy to see you arrive. You and the *kinner* are most *wilkom*, regardless of whether they are under my charge or you are simply visiting."

"In that case—" he grinned at her "—might you have any cookies to offer your visitor? I heard everyone raving about them at lunch, but I never got around to tasting one before I left."

"Sweets before supper? Tsk, tsk," Hannah said in mock consternation, and they both chuckled. "Please, take a seat and I'll fix coffee."

After the screen door slammed behind Hannah, Sawyer teetered nervously in the second rocking chair, running his fingers through his hair. He was glad he wore the fresh shirt Doris had laundered, and he smoothed the fabric down against his chest.

When Hannah returned, she told him a bit about her sister over the refreshments, and he talked about Gertrude and Kathryn.

"I can tell from the stories they share that the *kinner* adore Gertrude," Hannah remarked. "I hope to be that kind of *ant* to my sister's *bobbel*."

"I have every confidence you will be," Sawyer stated. He stammered before saying, "You mentioned my being ungrateful…and I, um, I want you to know how much I appreciate it that you are the one caring for my *kinner*."

"You pay me well," Hannah replied. "Too well, I think. But beyond payment, I am happy to do it. We are, after all, neighbors. For a time, anyway. I'd like to believe we are friends, as well."

"We are indeed," Sawyer declared vehemently, and then he immediately felt self-conscious. "As your friend—as your neighbor…that is, as your friendly neighbor, I want you to know if you are ever in need of *my* help, I hope you will ask me."

"Really?" she asked, laughing in her fetching manner. "Because there is something that would be helpful."

"What is it?"

"I will be right back," she said and collected the dishes. When she emerged from the house, she was carrying a wooden swing. "I'm too short to hang this on the willow, and *Groossdaadi's* balance is unreliable because of his hearing problem."

Sawyer laughed heartily. "I'm definitely the right man for this task."

He retrieved the ladder from the shed, and slight as she was, Hannah's firm grasp held it steady. But even before he ascended the ladder, he felt twelve feet tall.

Chapter Eight

Sarah was so delighted by the swing that when Hannah's grandfather entered the house for supper, she ran pell-mell toward him and wrapped her arms around his waist.

"I pumped so high I nearly kicked the clouds," she yelled, and although Hannah's grandfather couldn't see her mouth to read her lips, Hannah sensed he understood Sarah's elation.

He patted the top of her head and then squawked, "Bah," before loping away.

"Sarah swinged the longest," Samuel complained.

"I *swunged*," Sarah emphasized. "And I gave you both a turn."

Samuel ignored her, saying, "I want a longer turn after dinner."

"Actually," Hannah interrupted, "any *kinner* who don't quarrel during supper time will be allowed to take their *daed* to the stream when he arrives this evening."

"Really?" Simon questioned.

"Really. It's so muggy tonight I think your *daed* might appreciate the cool water."

Sawyer grinned when Hannah suggested it, and the children raced ahead, shouting, "This way, *Daed*!"

Before Sawyer and Hannah had a chance to remove their own shoes and socks, the triplets waded into the stream. Samuel, Sarah and Simon bent down, drawing water in their cupped hands. They formed a circle, their golden heads nearly touching as they studied their find.

"Look, *Daed*, there are bits of gold dust in the water," Sarah gasped.

"I think that must be mica," Sawyer answered, drawing nearer.

"*Neh*, it's gold. Come closer," Simon beckoned.

When Sawyer leaned in to get a look, the children splashed the water toward his face. "Surprise!" they yelled in concert.

He backed away and gave such a hearty laugh that droplets of water flew from his beard.

"Teacher showed us that trick," Simon said, doubling over.

"Oh, did she, now?" Sawyer asked. "Well, we'll see how she likes it." He lifted a handful at Hannah, who kicked water back toward him, squealing.

For the next hour, Sawyer overturned rocks and explored the banks with Hannah and the children, until Hannah heard a rumble.

"A storm is coming. We must hurry back," she warned.

"I think it's still in the distance," Sawyer said, just as a flash illuminated off the water.

"*Neh*, it's here. It's here!" she cried frantically. "Run!"

She swiped up her socks and shoes and then grabbed Sarah by the hand. "Get the boys," she hollered over her shoulder to Sawyer, who already had rounded them up and was close on her heels.

They raced toward the house against the gusty wind that drove the rain sideways into their skin like hot bullets. As they crossed the open field and sprinted up a slope, Hannah's bare feet slipped on the wet grass and she sprawled flat on her stomach on the ground. Above them, thunder crackled and a fork of lightning ripped the sky in two.

"Keep running! Get into the workshop," she urged Sarah. "Don't try to make it to the house!"

"Go!" Sawyer commanded the boys, thrusting his shoes into their hands.

He scooped Hannah into his arms and didn't stop running until he was safely inside her grandfather's workshop. Only then did she exhale, uncertain whether it was thunder or her own heartbeat that was reverberating so raucously in her ears.

Sawyer gently placed Hannah down, but as soon as her foot touched the floor, she winced.

"Wrap your arms around my neck," he said, shifting so she could reach. As he situated her onto a stool, he could feel her fluttering like a bird against his chest.

"Aw, look at this!" Simon stared in awe. The three children were mesmerized by a shelf of toys Hannah's grandfather had made. Sarah stood motionless in front of the dollhouse, her mouth agape.

"You may look, but don't touch," Sawyer instructed them. To Hannah he asked, "May I examine your foot?"

Although the light was waning, when he ran his rough hands over her elegant ankle, he peered into her eyes for a sign of pain. She flinched when a roar of thunder shook the little shed.

"Does that hurt?" he asked.

"Neh," she replied. "It wasn't that. I know I shouldn't be nervous because *Gott* protects as well as He provides, but these storms make me come unraveled."

Oh, so that's why she flinches at loud noises, Sawyer thought. *That, and her* groossdaadi's *voice.*

Sawyer cupped her heel in his hand and examined her ankle once again. "I think you only twisted it," he announced. "It's not even a sprain. It's not swelling."

"I'm so embarrassed," she admitted.

"Why? A twisted ankle can hurt as much as a sprain. You were charging quite fast when it happened. I imagine the pain shot through you like a knife."

"I'm embarrassed by my anxious behavior," she confessed. "What kind of role model am I for the *kinner*, to be afraid of thunderstorms?"

"The *kinner*, I'm sorry to say, aren't paying you any mind," he replied. "They're transfixed by the toys your *groossdaadi* created."

A clap of thunder so startled Hannah that she nearly toppled off the stool. Sawyer clasped her by her shoulders, helping her adjust her balance.

"I'm glad they aren't bothered by storms." She sighed. "I should have outgrown this fear as surely as I outgrew my childhood dresses, but some memories are more difficult to forget than others."

Thinking of Eliza's illness, Sawyer vigorously nodded in agreement. "Did you experience an unusually violent storm as a child?"

"Jah," she said, averting her eyes from his. Her lashes feathered her cheeks as she glanced down, wringing her hands. "A lightning strike brought down the tree that claimed my parents' lives."

"How frightful," Sawyer murmured sympathetically. After a pause, he nudged her elbow and joked, "But you're safe now. After all, I am the tallest one here. If lightning is to strike, it will strike me."

"Perish the thought!" she exclaimed. Her mortified expression made him laugh so hard that she began laughing, too—as did the children—and pretty soon, the raging storm had passed.

On Wednesday, Hannah's mailbox contained a letter addressed *Sarah Plank, c/o Hannah Lantz*. The return address indicated it was from Gertrude Plank, Sawyer's sister. Hannah was puzzled by why Gertrude would send the letter to her instead of in care of Sarah's uncle. Then she recalled when she was helping Sarah write a letter to Gertrude, she wasn't sure what John Plank's return address was, so she had scribbled her own address on the upper-left corner of the envelope.

She sat in the rocking chair while Sarah stood beside her on the porch. The boys were grateful Sarah was preoccupied with the mail because it gave them an opportunity to push each other on the swing without Sarah counting to one hundred—the maximum number of pushes she allowed her brothers per turn.

My dear niece Sarah,

What a wonderful surprise to receive a note from you! I'm glad your teacher, Hannah Lantz, helped you write it, and I am certain she will help you read this letter from me, as well.

Your initials look beautiful in cursive. I have always liked the letter *S* more than any other letter in cursive, although *L* is also lovely. You are very young to be learning cursive—do you know how to draw any other letters besides *S* and *P*? You will have to write again to show me.

Your aunt is feeling better, and the baby is slowly gaining weight. Her lungs are getting stronger, too. Now she sounds like a bleating lamb when she cries instead of like a mewling kitten. The midwife said she had never seen such a tiny baby before. We are blessed the Lord is increasing her size.

I am cooking for four men here—your uncle and

three hired hands. One of them, Seth Lambright, says my meat loaf is the best he's ever tasted.

I miss your smile, and Samuel and Simon's antics. Remember me to your father and tell him I will write to him next.

Your loving aunt,
Gertrude

Hannah read the letter aloud three times until Sarah had it memorized. She bounded down the stairs, waving the page at her brothers.

"Listen," she cried to them. "I will read this letter from Gertrude—she wrote a message for you, too!"

Hannah noticed there was a second sheet of paper folded inside the envelope. It was addressed *Postscript for Hannah*. She unfolded it and read:

Dear Hannah,

I am grateful you are taking such wonderful care of the children. I also appreciate the peace of mind and happiness you have brought Sawyer. He is slow to express his affection, but if you are patient enough to untangle my niece's hair, you have patience enough for him to prove me right.

Sincerely,
Gertrude Plank

Hannah read the note a second time. What a strange thing for Gertrude to write. She didn't recall helping Sarah write anything about her hair, and they certainly didn't mention anything about Sawyer in the letter.

She was warmed by Gertrude's complimenting her care for the children, but she dismissed the notion that she'd brought happiness to Sawyer's life as a sisterly expression of gratitude. It was the kind of thing little Sarah would do—minding her brothers' manners for them.

But there was no need for Gertrude to thank Hannah on behalf of Sawyer; he said as much each time he saw Hannah before school and after supper, often lingering to chat with her about the day's events or else to share a snack together with the children. The week flew by, and before Hannah knew it, it was Saturday—the day Sawyer invited her and her grandfather to come into town with them.

"I'd appreciate your help fitting the boys with shoes," he'd claimed. "This will also save your horse a trip, as I'm sure your *groossdaadi* has errands to run in town anyway."

"And we have a special surprise to share with you!" Simon announced.

"Shush!" Sarah admonished him.

Hannah didn't have any idea what surprise they had planned, but it hardly mattered: she considered time together with all of them to be time well spent, and it couldn't come soon enough.

Sawyer was perturbed. On Saturday morning, he received a letter from his foreman:

> Vernon Mast's injury hadn't yet healed, so I switched responsibilities with him as you directed. Unfortunately, Vernon's organizational skills don't match his talents as a carpenter. Subsequently, we missed two important deadlines—both for the Miller & Sons account—and we've botched several regional deliveries to boot.

Sawyer crumpled the paper in frustration and chucked it across the room. As frustrated as he was, he knew it wasn't Vernon's fault. Sawyer had put him in a position for which he was ill-suited, and now Sawyer needed to return to Ohio as quickly as possible to set things right with the customers and help his crew get back on schedule.

He realized that cutting his Saturday working hours in half by going into town wasn't going to speed things up on the farm any, but he had to get the boys new shoes. He was grateful for Hannah's attentiveness—he hadn't noticed how ill-fitting they were until she mentioned it.

He quickly penned a letter back to his foreman, telling him to resume the accounting and scheduling duties. "Prioritize the Miller & Sons orders. Give Vernon whatever woodworking projects he can handle and ask the other men to work late to take up any slack. I will, of course, compensate them for their time," he directed. "When I return, we'll consider hiring another man."

Sawyer hoped it didn't come to that, primarily because he didn't know any other men in his district who possessed the quality of skills the clients expected from his shop. He hated to admit it, but even among the Amish, he found the workmanship of the younger men to be sloppier than the standards he'd been raised to deliver.

His business dilemmas weighed heavily on his mind, especially since his decisions affected the livelihood of families beyond his own. He set his pen down with a heavy sigh and folded the paper into an envelope so he could drop it in a mailbox in town.

When he saw Hannah waving from the porch, a smile decorating her face, he momentarily forgot about his business problems in Ohio.

"It's a beautiful day, isn't it?" she asked as he approached, lifting her chin to scan his face.

Although it was as humid and overcast as ever, he agreed, "A beautiful day, indeed."

Hannah squeezed into the back of the buggy with the children, who sang songs along the way, while Sawyer and Hannah's grandfather took the front seat. When they arrived in town, the old man set off toward the hardware store, while the rest of them entered the *Englisch* clothing shop that carried the kinds of shoes the children needed.

"*Kumme*, Samuel," Sawyer beckoned the boy. "The clerk needs to measure your foot."

"That's Simon, not Samuel," Hannah whispered, nudging him.

"You're right—it is," chuckled Sawyer, lifting Simon's hat and brushing his hair away from his ear. "How can you tell when they are both dressed alike and wearing hats? Even I get mixed up unless I can see which one has the birthmark."

"A mother always knows her children," the *Englisch* salesclerk interjected.

Sawyer recognized that if the clerk assumed Hannah was the children's mother, she must have assumed Hannah was Sawyer's wife, as well. Glancing toward Hannah, he noticed her fair skin was splotching with pink, and she gave him a quick half smile. He couldn't interpret her expression for certain, but she didn't seem to be displeased and neither was he. Although he felt a small pang of disloyalty toward Eliza, Sawyer figured there was no harm done, and he didn't correct the woman's error.

As they were returning to the buggy, the children stopped in front of Schrock's Authentic Amish Shop.

"Look!" Samuel said excitedly, pointing to the window. "A train like the one in your *groossdaadi's* workshop."

Sawyer noticed it had a Model Only sign attached to

the caboose. "It looks as if it's not for sale," he noted, just as a short bespectacled man came out of the shop.

"*Guder nammidaag*, Hannah," Joseph Schrock greeted her in Pennsylvania Dutch. Hannah introduced him to everyone in turn.

"I'm happy to see you," Joseph said. "All of your *groossdaadi's* toys sold! A busload of tourists came in and bought up every last one, except the display model, which we kept for future business. Several people asked to order more and have them delivered in time for Christmas. My *daed* was so pleased he cleared an extra space for double the toys and the dollhouse besides! Is Albert in town today?"

"He is," Hannah hedged. "But, Joseph, you know he never goes back on his word."

Joseph's shoulders drooped. "Please, will you talk to him for me?"

"I will try," Hannah agreed, her expression melancholy.

When they had made their way down the street, the children galloping ahead of them, Hannah explained the situation about the toys and her grandfather's promise never to step foot inside Schrock's shop again.

"I feel terrible disappointing Joseph, but when *Groossdaadi* says *never*, there is absolutely no changing his mind."

"But this could be a source of steady income," Sawyer protested.

"*Jah*, but *Gott* will provide us what we need," Hannah said with a sigh.

"*Gott* already *is* providing you what you need," Sawyer argued. "And your *groossdaadi* is rejecting it. What kind of man would rather have you work like a mule than swallow his pride?"

Hannah's temper flared. "Work *like a mule*?" she asked, appalled. Certainly he'd never use such a phrase about a woman who was a mother of her own children. "Is a beast what you'd compare me to? Is that what you think of a woman who teaches other people's *kinner*? Or who cares for them? Is that what you think of *me*?"

"That isn't what I meant at all," Sawyer replied. "It was just a figure of speech."

Hannah turned her head to the side and controlled her voice so as not to upset the children, but she was shaking as she said, "Who are you to criticize the way in which my *groossdaadi* and I run our household? What concern is it to you, Sawyer Plank?"

"It isn't any concern of mine," Sawyer said, gritting his teeth. "It isn't any concern at all. Forget I said anything."

They walked side by side in silence. Tears and fury blurred Hannah's vision so that she walked crookedly, nearly bumping into Samuel, who had stopped in front of the *Englisch* ice-cream shop and was holding open the door for her.

"We're here," he said excitedly.

"It's our surprise for you!" Sarah exclaimed.

Simon gave a little hop. "*Daed* is treating us all to an ice-cream cone, double scoop. They make it homemade here!"

Hannah winced. Her stomach was tied in such tight knots, she didn't know how she could eat, but the children were so pleased with themselves, she couldn't say no. Sawyer asked what flavor her grandfather preferred and then purchased him a dish of maple walnut. Everyone else chose strawberry, in honor of Hannah.

"It's like eating pink snow instead of pink sunshine, isn't it, Hannah?" Samuel asked.

"It is just like that," Hannah replied. "What a *gut* use of metaphor, Samuel."

The youngsters darted ahead as the adults lagged behind, not speaking. When they got to the hitch, her grandfather was nowhere in sight, so the children plopped down on a grassy knoll while Hannah and Sawyer stood waiting at the buggy.

Hannah could barely stomach her ice cream, but the more she prolonged eating it, the more it began to drip. She tipped her head to lick a pink rivulet running down the side of the cone. It was useless; her manners were no better than Doris Hooley's. But what did she care what Sawyer Plank thought of her anyway?

"Hannah," he began, after he had finished crunching the last bit of his cone and swiped a napkin across his mouth.

"What is it?" she asked impatiently, fixing her attention on her ice cream.

"There are two things I need you to hear," Sawyer stated definitively.

"Go on, then." She shrugged, licking her cone in a deliberately indifferent manner.

"The first is that I am very sorry. I didn't mean to insult you or your *groossdaadi*. All I meant was that I would expect a man who cares for you to value you so much he'd do anything within his power to share your burdens, or die trying."

Hannah felt her insides melt as surely as the ice cream she was holding. No man had ever said such a thing about her value to her before. She glanced under her lashes at him, afraid to trust her voice to speak. "And what is the second thing you want to tell me?"

Relieved that Hannah seemed to have accepted his apology, Sawyer gained confidence. He reached forward to touch her face with his napkin. "The second thing is that you have a dab of strawberry ice cream on your nose and another on your chin."

Her laughter was as melodic to his ears as a bubbling brook and twice as refreshing. He readily joined in as she blotted her face with her own napkin.

"Did I get it all?" she asked.

"All but this spot here," he said, cupping her face in his fingers. Her skin was so porcelain and her features so dainty, he felt as clumsy as if he were handling fine china when he brushed her chin with his thumb. Their eyes locked for a long moment, and Sawyer felt his breathing quicken.

"Time to go!" a loud voice shouted behind him, and Sawyer immediately dropped his hand.

He retrieved the container of ice cream and plastic spoon he had set on the seat of the buggy and presented it to Hannah's grandfather, who batted it away. Its contents tipped, landing upside down on the ground.

"Unlike with my granddaughter, my affections cannot be bought," he muttered, climbing into the buggy.

Hannah ducked her head and stepped back. Clapping to get the children's attention, she called them to the buggy. Sawyer himself felt like a scolded child as he climbed in after Hannah's grandfather. Oblivious to the tension, Sarah, Simon and Samuel sang all the way home. Sawyer half expected the old man to demand they stop singing out of pure spite, but instead he sat in stony silence.

When they arrived, Hannah's grandfather trudged to the house, as the three children spilled from the buggy. Sawyer immediately directed them back into it.

"Aren't we going to eat supper with Hannah?" Simon asked.

"Not tonight," he said. "Doris Hooley said she would come by today and prepare enough for all."

"But she always wants to brush my hair," Sarah whimpered. "It hurts the way she does it."

"*Kumme*, get into the buggy!" Sawyer called, and the children obeyed.

"I'm sorry" was all Sawyer could think to say to Hannah.

"You needn't be," she replied firmly, and he knew she meant it. "For anything."

He watched as Hannah crossed the lawn. Before disappearing into the house, she turned and waved, calling, "I will see you Monday, *Gott* willing."

Chapter Nine

Hannah never scrubbed the floors as thoroughly as she did when she was angry, and on Saturday afternoon she was so mad, the wood gleamed.

Why did her grandfather have to behave that way? It seemed as if he'd intentionally been trying to snuff out any flicker of happiness she experienced—especially in the company of young men—since she was a teenager, and he showed no signs of stopping now that she was an adult. But why? What had overtaken him, to make him act so hostile toward Sawyer? And how dare he say her affections could be bought—as if she had ever had her head turned by worldly riches! None of it made sense, and she refused to feel guilty for having accepted the rare luxury of a store-bought ice-cream cone—or a kind expression of support—from Sawyer.

For the next hour, her grandfather refused to come out of his bedroom. At first, Hannah was so incensed by his rude display in town that after she fixed supper, instead of telling him it was ready, she turned the pot to simmer and went to retrieve the mail. Among the items in her mailbox was a letter from Eve. She settled into the rocking chair on the porch and ran her finger under the flap of the envelope.

"Dearest Hannah," the letter began.

I know such topics are usually left unsaid, but I must confide that the baby has been kicking and somersaulting constantly! I think it is from this hot weather. I cannot wait to become a mother. I thought no love could be deeper than the love I felt for my husband, but I already love this child with my whole being.

Here, Hannah paused. As happy as she was that her sister was married and with child, it pained her to be reminded of what she hadn't ever experienced and probably never would, if her grandfather's abrasive attitude didn't change. She took a breath and kept reading.

I enjoyed hearing about the Plank children and their father, Sawyer. Is he really as tall as you described, or might he appear head and shoulders above the rest in your eyes for another reason?

Confused by her sister's question, Hannah again stopped reading. Eve had always been closely attuned to Hannah's feelings, and she wondered what she'd written that may have caused her sister to think she saw Sawyer as larger-than-life.

I am glad you and Grandfather have another source of income—as long as he doesn't run Sawyer over with the buggy! How humiliating that must have been for you.

Hannah sighed. Her sister's simple comment showed she remembered what it was like to live with her grandfather's unpredictable behavior. But an uncharacteristic misgiving popped into Hannah's mind: at least Eve had escaped.

Eve closed the letter by writing, "Please pray God provides continued health for the baby and for me."

Again, a bitter thought flitted through Hannah's heart. Why should she ask God for provision for Eve when her sister already had all she could ever need?

She lowered her eyelids and inhaled deeply, willing herself not to cry. With her big toe, she pushed the rocker back and forth, dawdling until she felt composed enough to enter the house and serve her grandfather supper.

Because he wasn't seated at the table or resting in his chair in the parlor, she entered his room and found him lying in bed, feverish, the covers pulled to his chin. His breathing was labored, and he shook from a chill. He looked so infirmed, she immediately was contrite about how furious she had been. For the rest of the evening and through the night, each time she entered the room to change his compress or give him a sip of tea or broth, Hannah knelt by his bedside, praying for him to get well again.

By Sunday morning, his fever hadn't broken, although he dressed and sat with Hannah in the sitting room for Scripture reading and prayer, since it was an "off Sunday," and there was no church meeting that week. Afterward, he stumbled toward his bedroom, and Hannah quickly wrapped his arm around her shoulder and supported his weight as he lumbered down the hall. When she had arranged his pillows around his head, she reached to draw the shades, but he grasped her hand.

"Don't leave me, Gloria," he said, his eyes wild.

That was her grandmother's name. Hannah fretted he was confused from the fever.

"I'll be right back," she mouthed. "I am only going to get you a fresh glass of water."

"Neh," her grandfather pleaded. "Don't leave me."

Hannah blinked back her tears, realizing he was afraid she'd leave him for good, like her grandmother did when she died. Perhaps he feared Sawyer would offer to hire her to go and care for the children in Ohio once her teaching job ended. The children had mentioned having a *daadi haus* on their property—separate living quarters would have made the arrangement appropriate. That must have been why he was unspeakably rude to Sawyer—he was afraid Sawyer had intentions of taking her away from him, leaving him here all alone.

"*Groossdaadi*," she promised solemnly, looking into his eyes, "I would never leave you."

Satisfied, he closed his eyes and fell into a deep slumber. Hannah pulled the shades, leaving just enough light so she could see to read the Bible, which she did for over an hour. Eventually, she stretched and peeked out the window.

Whom did she expect to arrive for a Sunday visit? Eve and her husband would have let her know if they planned a trip. Jacob, Miriam and Abigail wouldn't drop by because Miriam was limiting her activities. Doris had frequented their home on off Sundays, but it was more likely she was at the Plank farm today, trying to capture Sawyer's attention. As for Sawyer, Hannah felt she'd be fortunate if her grandfather hadn't frightened him away permanently.

She sighed and flipped a page in her Bible. What was wrong with her? Usually she was content to spend a Sabbath resting and reading or in prayer, but today she felt at odds. No wonder her grandfather was concerned she'd abandon him: it was terribly lonely not to be in the company of people who cared about you and whom you cared about, too.

Her grandfather stirred, coughing. She touched his

arm—his skin was damp with sweat, and she knew his fever had broken.

"What are you doing here?" he asked in a groggy voice.

"I was making sure you don't feel as lonely as I do," she said. Knowing he couldn't read her lips in the dusky light, she gave his arm a reassuring pat.

"I am hungry," he demanded, and she knew any hint of vulnerability he'd shown was gone. But she'd already made up her mind she'd stay home with him on Monday, just to be certain he was back to his usual grumpy self.

Come Monday morning, it was Doris, not Hannah, who stood at the top step of the schoolhouse stairs.

"*Guder mariye*, Sawyer," she said. "Sarah, Simon and Samuel, you and the other *kinner* will be in my classroom today."

"Did something happen?" Sawyer asked, panic rising in his voice. "Is Hannah alright?"

"You are as much of a nervous Nellie as she is," Doris said with a giggle. "Hannah is fine. It's her *groossdaadi* who is ill. She must have come here early this morning, because I found a note from her on my desk, along with her scholars' lesson plans."

"I see," Sawyer said, feeling both relieved she was alright and disappointed she wasn't present.

"She left a note for you, as well. You'll have to forgive me for reading it—I thought it was meant for me."

Doris extended a folded piece of paper to Sawyer, who snatched it from her grasp.

"Sawyer," it said. "Grandfather has been ill since Saturday evening. He is on the mend, but I want to stay with him to tend to his care. If Doris agrees, might she take the children to the farm after school and watch them there until you are finished in the fields? This arrangement seems best. Hannah."

As soon as Sawyer glanced up from the letter, Doris batted her lashes and said, "I'm happy to bring the *kinner* home from school and tend to their care. I'll cook supper, as well."

Sawyer hesitated. What had Hannah meant by *This arrangement seems best*? It was only for this afternoon, right? Perhaps this one time he should pick the children up himself and take them directly to the farm? But that would mean he'd lose valuable working hours, and they weren't as far along as he'd hoped they'd be.

"Don't be shy." Doris gave Sawyer a nudge while he was silently mulling over his options. "It would be my pleasure."

"Denki," he agreed reluctantly. Then, so there would be no misunderstanding, he added, "I am certain Hannah's *groossdaadi* will recover and tomorrow she will take charge of the *kinner* once again."

But he didn't feel certain at all.

Over a light breakfast on Monday morning, Hannah relayed Joseph Schrock's offer to expand the amount of shelf space her grandfather would be allotted if he'd reconsider consigning his toys at the shop.

"Final means final!" her grandfather brayed, adamant that he'd never again conduct business with the Schrock family.

He puttered out to his shed to work on the cradle for Miriam and Jacob's baby, leaving Hannah to tackle her housework and laundering.

Although Hannah knew the children would be fine with Doris at the farm, and she wanted to prove to her grandfather that her primary commitment was to his well-being, by midday, she was eager to get back to her usual routine at school.

She missed all of her scholars and regretted having even one less day to spend with them before her class was combined with Doris's after harvest ended. Not to mention how much she missed spending the afternoon with the Plank children.

Also, she had to admit—at least to herself—she especially missed the few minutes of conversation she and Sawyer engaged in whenever they saw each other. It never seemed to matter whether they talked about the children's schoolwork, the weather or what they had for dinner, and she derived equal pleasure from watching his forehead crease with thoughtfulness or his eyes sparkle in good humor. Was that the emotion she somehow conveyed in her letter to Eve that made her sister perceive she held an exaggerated regard for Sawyer? Whatever the feeling she had around Sawyer was, Hannah couldn't deny longing to experience it again.

She was so gleeful to return to school on Tuesday she didn't mind at all that Doris jabbered on and on while Hannah wrote sums on the blackboard.

"I am itching to tell you something," Doris warbled. "But you must keep it a secret."

Hannah didn't want to participate in Doris's gossip. "If it's something that's not supposed to be shared, perhaps you shouldn't mention it," she advised.

"But I must," she insisted. "It is too *wunderbaar* to keep to myself. I am being courted!"

"What?" Hannah gasped incredulously.

"*Jah*, it officially happened when he asked me yesterday, after I took the *kinner* to the farm."

Hannah couldn't believe what she was hearing. She knew Sawyer was sorry for the remarks he'd made about

Doris, but she never imagined he'd come to think so highly of her that he'd actually court her. She felt as if she had been socked in the gut, but she choked out the words. "How nice for you and Sawyer."

"Sawyer?" Doris jeered. "Who said anything about Sawyer? I'm being courted by his *onkel*, John Plank. What would make you think I'd be interested in that cold fish Sawyer? In fact, he seems more *your* type than mine."

Hannah winced at Doris's crass insult. "I don't think he's a cold fish at all," she retorted. "But I'm not interested in being courted. My responsibility is to my *groossdaadi*."

"One day your *groossdaadi* will die," Doris said frankly. "And you will be past marrying age—or at least, past childbearing age. That's why John and I are so delighted to have kindled a relationship now. Odd, how we never considered each other in the years since his wife died. In a way, if it weren't for his breaking his leg, our courtship might have never occurred. The Lord works in mysterious ways, *jah*?"

"Jah," Hannah agreed.

Yet as she moved into the entryway to greet the students, Hannah was pestered by jabs of envy. Why didn't the Lord work in mysterious ways for her? He seemed to provide for everyone else—even providing a match for someone as bold and overbearing as Doris Hooley! What about Hannah's provision? The one provision she desired so deeply she scarcely could allow herself to admit it, much less to ask for it anymore?

Just then, the children made their way up the walkway, with Sawyer several yards behind them. Watching them approach, Hannah rationalized that she, too, had everything she needed in that moment. Today, she would serve the students and serve God in her role as their teacher.

Then she would care for the Plank children as if they were her own. If she was fortunate, she'd have a few extra moments to converse with Sawyer alone. For now, she had her daily bread.

"Teacher!" Sarah gushed. "How we missed you yesterday!"

"Guder mariye," Hannah greeted them, a smile spreading across her face. "I am very glad to see you, too. You may put your books at your desks and go play outside before the bell is rung."

"*Guder mariye*, Hannah," Sawyer said as the children cantered out the door. "How is your *groossdaadi*?"

"After a few days of rest, he is as healthy as a horse. But he's not any more polite, I'm afraid. Sometimes when he's coming down with an illness, his manners aren't what they should be, and I apologize."

"I'm glad to hear that," Sawyer replied. "I mean, I am glad to hear about the improvement in his health, not about his manners."

When Hannah giggled, Sawyer wasn't sure if it was because he'd bumbled his words or because he'd made a joke—but he didn't care; he just delighted in the sound.

He continued, "You needn't excuse him on my account. I took no offense. I was more concerned that you might have borne the brunt of his…his discontent after we left. So, how are you?"

"I am glad to be back at school," she admitted. Then, with a faraway note in her voice, she said, "I'm glad the *kinner* are coming home with me after school today. I truly missed their presence yesterday. Without them, I felt… I don't know. I guess I might say I was at a loss."

Sawyer was flooded with a sense of warmth. "I was concerned your *groossdaadi* might not have wanted you to care for the *kinner* any longer," he ventured. "I didn't know what I would have done without you."

Hannah scrunched her eyebrows together. "Didn't Doris take *gut* care of them?"

"*Jah*, she did. Very *gut* care," Sawyer immediately replied. The last thing he wanted to do was to inadvertently insult Doris again, especially not when she was within earshot. He lowered his voice. "It's just that she's not..."

When he didn't finish his sentence, Hannah inclined her head to meet his eyes. "She's not what?" she asked. "She's not a *gut* cook?"

"Neh, neh," Sawyer protested. "She made a delicious supper."

"Did you mean she's not kind?" Hannah persisted. "Or that she's not helpful?"

After each question, Sawyer shook his head. His ears were burning, but he didn't know how to change the subject or distract Hannah.

"She's not *what*?" she emphasized again, before impishly asking, "She's not *short*?"

"That's true—she's definitely not short." Sawyer guffawed, savoring the twinkle in Hannah's eye. "And neither am I. But that's not what I was going to say."

"Then what exactly *were* you going to say?" Hannah teased, a saucy smirk on her lips.

He leaned forward, so as not to be overheard. "I was going to say, 'She's not *you*,'" he answered in a husky voice.

Hannah's mouth puckered into an O and her cheeks blossomed with pink. For a change, it was she, not Sawyer, who appeared to be tongue-tied. Before either of them had a chance to say anything more, Doris bustled into the room.

"Hello, you two," she chirped. "You both look as guilty

as *kinner* caught with their hands in the cookie jar! You haven't been sharing a secret, have you?"

"Not at all," Hannah responded, giving Sawyer a furtive wink. "Sawyer was just telling me about the *wunderbaar* supper you made the other evening."

"I'm glad you enjoyed it, Sawyer." Doris beamed. "Because as you know, we're meeting at your *onkel's* house for church this Sunday and I have agreed to prepare dinner for everyone. I was about to ask Hannah if she'd help with the dinner preparations, too."

"Of course," Hannah agreed. "It's the least I can do, especially since *Groossdaadi* and I never host because we don't have a big enough gathering room. Sarah will assist me. Now, let's call the scholars in for school, shall we? It's past time."

Sawyer recognized a hint when he heard one, just as he recognized the quality of his exchange with Hannah had crossed the line from *friendly* to *flirtatious*. He hadn't intended for it to happen, but as the buggy sailed toward the farm, he realized he wasn't exactly sorry that it had.

For the rest of the week, temperatures hit record-breaking highs for September. It was so stifling in the tiny schoolhouse that Hannah frequently delivered the lessons outside on the grass beneath the willow tree, where at least there was a small rustle of hot breeze. Yet she hardly minded the unseasonal heat; it gave the illusion that it was still summer. She wanted time to stand still so she wouldn't have to think about harvest ending or saying goodbye to her scholars and to the Plank family. Especially now that Sawyer revealed how special she was to them—in particular, how special she was to *him*.

"He didn't use that exact phrase, but surely that was what he meant. Why else would he have been so embarrassed when he finally spoke the words?" she wrote in a letter to Eve on Thursday after dinner. She had been alternately elated and befuddled ever since her conversation with Sawyer on Tuesday.

In the next sentence, she contradicted herself.

Oh, who am I to think Sawyer Plank has any romantic feelings toward me? He probably only meant I was unique compared with Doris in the way I care for the children, or because of the relationship I have with *them*, not with *him*.

Sawyer and I haven't had another opportunity to speak to each other alone again since Tuesday, as the children have always been close at hand, so I cannot gauge what he might be feeling at this time. I'm afraid I'm better at reading the emotions of children than those of adults—especially men.

It hardly matters anyway, does it? At the end of harvest, Sawyer will return to Ohio and I will stay with Grandfather.

Yet I must confess, my dear sister, I long for a fraction of what you describe between you and your husband. Try as I have to suppress it, it is still something I yearn to experience. I would welcome the affections of a man about whom I feel the same for any period of time, even a brief season.

Please pray that I wouldn't envy those who have what I don't. I know envy is a sin, and I loathe the way I feel when I am envious.

After rereading her words, Hannah deliberated about whether or not to tear up the page. Such intimate romantic matters were seldom discussed, even among sisters. But Hannah didn't know how else to make sense of her emotions since she'd never before experienced feelings like these. She was in such a daze, she didn't hear her grandfather enter the parlor.

"The buggy needs extensive repair," he announced loudly. "I will speak to Turner King about it tomorrow."

"But why? What happened?"

The buggy was old, but as of two days ago, it was operating well. Why would it suddenly need *extensive repair*? When her grandfather left the room without responding, she shuddered.

He must have had a collision when he went to town this week. More likely, he *caused* a collision. She briefly considered tromping out to the garage to see the damage herself, but then decided against it. It was almost dark, and besides, seeing it would only upset her, especially if it was severe. Her grandfather was unharmed, and she assumed the other driver was, too, which was all that really mattered.

Yet her heart sank, knowing the repair costs would far outweigh whatever her grandfather earned for the cradle and rocker he was making for Miriam and Jacob. She picked her pen back up and inscribed a final line: "And please pray that the Lord will continue to provide for our daily needs, which are abundant."

Usually just the sight of Hannah's lithe form and graceful movements enlivened Sawyer's spirit, but on Friday morning when he arrived at the schoolhouse, his mind was preoccupied with the letter he had received from his foreman the day before. Because of continued mix-ups with recent deliveries, their biggest *Englisch* customer was threatening to terminate their professional association.

Hannah sent Simon, Samuel and Sarah off to carry books and a blanket to the lawn beneath the willow for morning lessons. She then turned to Sawyer, squinting.

"You seem troubled this morning," she said. "Is the heat getting to you, or is it something else? Are you ill?"

She looked so distressed herself, Sawyer found himself disclosing details of the situation he normally would have kept to himself because he didn't want her to fret about his health.

"Oh!" Hannah exclaimed when he had finished. "How terrible! What are you going to do?"

"There isn't much I can do from here," he stated. "As soon as possible, I'll need to return to set things straight again."

Hannah nodded, her blue eyes clouded. "Is there anything I can do to help?"

She appeared so unsettled, he was torn between not wanting to say anything else and feeling as if a huge burden had been lifted from his shoulders simply by telling her what had been weighing on his mind.

"Jah," he replied. "You could pray about it for me, but please don't mention it to anyone else—I don't want John to find out. He's already pushing himself to do more than he ought to do physically in an effort to help with the harvest. If he hears about this, he'll insist that the boys can handle it from here, and he'll send me home straightaway. I don't think they're quite ready for that."

"I won't say a word," Hannah agreed, and when she solemnly blinked her eyelashes, his knees felt like jelly. "Except to the Lord in prayer. I am certain He will provide a solution. But I'm sorry this has happened."

"And if it weren't upsetting enough," Sawyer continued, suddenly feeling free enough to pour his heart out to Hannah, "I received a letter from my sister Gertrude. She wishes to stay in Indiana a bit longer. She says it's to help my sister Kathryn, who was quite ill after the birth of the *bobbel*, but I suspect it's because a young man there may be courting her."

"Seth," Hannah murmured, a knowing look on her face.

"What?" Sawyer was taken aback. *"Who?"*

Hannah didn't elaborate. Instead, she asked, "Why is it so upsetting that Gertrude is helping your other sister?"

"Because *I* will need her help with the *kinner* as soon as I return."

"Could you hire someone to mind them before and after school?" Hannah inquired. "Look how well it's worked out for me to provide care for them."

"It has worked well," Sawyer admitted. "There's no doubt about that. But it wouldn't work with someone else, not for the long haul. Besides, it's not as if Kathryn really needs help. She has fewer *kinner* than I and a husband, too. Their district is large and there are many young women available for hire. As I said, I suspect Gertrude is only making an excuse to stay there longer because she is interested in a young man. She ought not abandon her family for such frivolity."

"Do you consider a chance at love to be a frivolity?" Hannah asked quietly.

"I don't consider it to be a necessity."

"Perhaps Gertrude does."

"At her age, that is foolishness!" argued Sawyer.

"You remind me of my *groossdaadi*, who always said the same thing to me," Hannah retorted, her chin in the air. "Now if you'll excuse me, I need to get ready for class."

She swiveled and disappeared into the schoolhouse so quickly he didn't even get the chance to say goodbye.

What did I say? he wondered. And how did he manage to bungle the one thing that was going smoothly in his life?

Chapter Ten

Hannah numbly made it through the school day. If ever she had any inkling that Sawyer might feel toward her the way she felt toward him, he had thoroughly shattered it with his remarks. Clearly he thought of her as a nanny only—a very competent nanny, more so than Doris, but still just a nanny.

It took every ounce of determination to focus on the lessons. She was as wilted by her disappointment as the students were by the heat. For the last half hour of the day, she distributed colored pencils and paper for drawing and then sat mindlessly doodling at her own desk, too languid to do anything else.

She was relieved when classes were dismissed and she sent Sarah, Simon and Samuel outside for a moment so she could pack up her paperwork for the weekend. Just as she slid the last folder into her satchel, Doris pranced into the room.

"How can you move about so briskly in this weather? I'm sweltering."

"Lately, I feel as if I'm floating on a cloud," Doris replied. Her singsong reference to being courted by John Plank caused Hannah to feel even more dejected. "You haven't forgotten about making snitz pies for Sunday, have you?" she inquired.

"Of course not," Hannah confirmed. "I have a surplus

of dried apples prepared, and Sarah and I will bake the pies tomorrow. I'll send most of them home with Sawyer when he picks up the *kinner* tomorrow evening. However, I will need assistance bringing the rest to the Planks' farm. Our buggy is being repaired, so my *groossdaadi* and I will need a ride to services."

"It's no bother for me to give you a ride to and from the Plank farm," Doris offered. "Although I was hoping you could stay until everyone has left to help with the cleanup. Perhaps Joseph Schrock could give your *groossdaadi* a ride home after dinner, since your house is on his way?"

"Hmm." Hannah hesitated. "I think Turner King might have room in his buggy for *Groossdaadi* on the return trip instead."

"Just remember, you mustn't breathe a word of my secret about John and me to anyone."

Hannah snickered to herself that Doris probably had told most everyone in Willow Creek already anyway, but she agreed not to mention it.

No sooner did Doris leave the room than Jacob Stoltzfus entered.

"*Guder nammidaag*, Hannah." His face looked grim.

"*Guder nammidaag*, Jacob. Is something the matter?" she asked. She knew Abigail was playing in the yard with the Plank children, so her thoughts raced to Jacob's wife. "Is Miriam alright?"

"*Jah*, she is alright for now," Jacob confided. "The *bobbel* is alright, too. But the midwife saw us today and advised Miriam to restrict her activities even further. Which is why I have come to speak to you. We have an important matter we'd like you to consider."

"Of course. What is it?"

"Once harvest is over and your teaching is finished, might you help care for Miriam and oversee the household, including taking Abigail back and forth to school, while I am at the factory? We probably can't pay you as well as Sawyer Plank does, but since you are in need of employment and we are in need of help, it may be an opportune arrangement."

Hannah swallowed hard. She was simultaneously filled with concern for Miriam and Jacob and their unborn child, and with a sense of dread. True, she needed an income, but did God's provision for her have to involve running the household of the woman whose life *she* might have lived if she had agreed to marry Jacob Stolzfus?

Not that she ever wanted to marry him, but that was exactly the point. How was it that she now found herself in a position of overseeing Jacob's household when that was something she deliberately turned down years ago?

"I will speak to my *groossdaadi* about it," she answered. "Please know I am praying for you. Remember me to Miriam."

On the walk home, Hannah was quiet as she thought about Miriam and Jacob. As the children continued their quest to sneak up on late-season turtles in the stream, she perched on the embankment, dipping her feet in the current. She reclined against the grassy edge and noticed a handful of leaves overhead were yellowing around their edges. It may have felt like summer, but autumn was coming. She mused that for better or worse, life was always changing.

As the coolness of the water refreshed her skin, she felt a sense of rejuvenation washing over her spirit, too. Considering Miriam and Jacob's situation further, she recognized what a blessing it was that Eve and her baby were healthy. She couldn't imagine what a difficult time this was for Miriam and Jacob, especially after all they'd been through.

She asked herself how she could have been so filled

with envy for what she didn't have instead of filled with gratitude for what she did. Didn't she just write to Eve, asking her to pray that the Lord would provide their daily bread? And hadn't He done just that? Who was she to request something different, or something more? From this point on, she was going to joyfully appreciate all of His blessings, in whatever form they arrived, for however long they lasted. And if that included a passing crush on Sawyer Plank, she would welcome it with open arms!

With a new vigor, she leaped up from where she was reclining and waded out to join the children.

Sawyer's shirt clung to him like a second skin, and his grimy hair was matted around his forehead. He didn't want to say anything else to upset Hannah, and now he figured he had the perfect excuse for keeping his distance. But when he arrived to retrieve the children, she beckoned to him from the porch.

"*Kumme*, sit." She gestured. "Have a glass of lemonade. You look as if you could use it."

"Denki," he replied. He was relieved that whatever he'd said to aggravate her earlier in the day seemed to have passed. However, he still allowed her to direct the conversation.

She gestured toward the children on the swing. "It was too tropical this afternoon for swinging, so I promised them they could take their turns of one hundred pushes each in the cooler evening hours."

"I see," he acknowledged. After a moment of observation, he pointed out, "Look, it takes both of them to budge Samuel. He is finally gaining weight, thanks to you. They all are."

"It must be the bountiful sweets I feed them at school." Hannah sniggled, so Sawyer knew she was making light.

You're definitely a bountifully sweet teacher, Sawyer thought. Or did he voice the comment aloud? He wasn't sure. The children's blond heads were the only part of them that he could distinguish in the shadow of the willow, and the evening took on a nostalgic glow. He wished Eliza could have seen how big the children had gotten, yet he was grateful Hannah was there to appreciate this aspect of their childhood.

Sawyer didn't want to break the mood, nor did he want to give in to it. Hannah's presence in their family had undeniably awakened emotions in him he wasn't sure he was ready to experience. After a spell of silence, he cleared his throat.

"That's past one hundred!" he called. "*Kumme*, Sarah, off the swing. You need to be up early tomorrow to help Hannah with the baking."

Physically depleted as he was, Sawyer thought he would have dropped off to sleep the moment his head hit the pillow later that evening, but instead he lay blinking at the ceiling.

He wondered what had troubled Hannah earlier in the day and why it so suddenly lifted. Was she prone to moodiness?

He tried to think about what kinds of things caused Eliza to retreat from conversation, but he couldn't recall. Just thinking about his departed wife made him realize his memories of her weren't exactly fading, but they were changing. When he remembered them, they didn't cause as much loneliness as they once did. There were times when he couldn't picture her face as vividly, either. Even Sarah looked more like him than she did Eliza, although every now and then she'd assume a stance or make a gesture that was exactly like something her mother would have done.

His body ached, and he figured he must be overly tired

or getting old. Either way, as he drifted to sleep, the only face he pictured was Hannah's.

"Now remember," Sarah said to the boys after their father delivered the children to Hannah on Saturday morning, "you mustn't be underfoot in the kitchen. We have many pies to bake, and you can't be creating a ruckus."

"How could we forget?" Simon complained. "You've been talking about it for days."

"Jah," Samuel chimed in. "It's as if you think you're the only one who does anything helpful for Hannah."

"You're all helpful," Hannah contradicted. "In fact, I have a very important mission for you boys. I need you to run to the coop and gather eggs, or Sarah and I won't have enough for the crusts. Here's a pail and cloth. Please be very careful not to jostle them."

As they shot out of the kitchen, Sarah rolled her eyes and said with a sigh, *"Buwe"*—meaning *boys*—and Hannah had to turn her back so the girl wouldn't see her chuckle.

"Now, now, enough of that," she instructed. Over her shoulder she said, "If you have washed your hands, you may help me measure the flour for the crusts. We'll do that over here as soon as I bring—"

She was about to say "as soon as I bring the sack to the table," but when she turned to face Sarah, she saw the girl was attempting to lift the flour from the counter herself.

"Careful—it's open!" she warned, lunging to assist her, but it was too late. The heft of the sack was too much for Sarah, and as she doubled over trying to balance it, its contents spilled forward onto the floor.

"Oh, *neh*!" Hannah cried.

Sarah managed to keep it cradled in her arms until she reached the table. She hoisted it up the best she could, but at the last second, she dropped it onto the surface. It landed upside down with a plop and a *poof* of white. The powder covered her face and hair, and she stood in stunned silence, blinking.

At that second, from the yard one of the boys screamed, "Run!"

Hannah recognized the level of fear in his voice and bolted out the door and across the lawn in time to see her grandfather chasing something from the chicken coop with a shovel. Simon and Samuel hightailed it toward the porch, which Samuel reached first, but he stumbled on the top step and the pail flew from his grasp. Inches behind, Simon couldn't halt soon enough to keep from tripping over him. A tangle of elbows and knees and broken eggs, the boys scrambled through the door on their hands and knees.

Hannah rushed to their side. "There, there," she comforted them after confirming they were more frightened than injured. "Whatever happened?"

"At first, I thought it was a cat." Simon wept. "A strange black cat with short little legs."

"It had very sharp teeth," Samuel added. "It screeched at us."

"A fisher cat was after the eggs," Hannah's grandfather stated. She was so troubled about the children, she didn't notice him come in. "He got four of the *hinkel* and would have gone after the *kinner*, too."

Hannah gulped. She knew how ferocious fisher cats could be, and she thanked the Lord that her grandfather had been around to ward it off.

"But how did you know?" she asked. He had headed to his workshop earlier than usual that morning—right after he'd told her the astronomical sum Turner King estimated it would cost to repair the buggy. It was impossible for him to have heard either the animal's or the boys' cries.

"Bah, I keep an eye out" was all he said. He left the way he came, sidestepping the broken eggs on the porch.

Sarah called from the other room, "Are Simon and Samuel alright? Remind them not to come into the kitchen—I am still sweeping up the flour, and I don't want them traipsing through it."

"We'll need that broom out here when you're done." Hannah sighed and picked a piece of eggshell from Samuel's hair.

"Why?" Sarah appeared in the doorway, her hands on her hips. "What did those rascals do now?"

When the boys saw their sister's face covered in flour, they rolled on the floor where they lay, laughing and clutching their sides.

"Stop that! Stop that right now!" Sarah demanded, stomping her foot and bursting into tears.

Surveying the situation around her, Hannah honestly didn't know whether to join the boys in laughing or to cry alongside Sarah herself.

Shortly before Sawyer, Jonas and Phillip broke for lunch, John hobbled to the fields to assess their progress.

"You've made quite a bit of headway. Won't be more than three to four weeks now."

Sawyer was actually hoping to finish quicker than that, but he jested, "*Gott* willing, you'll be back on your feet by then if you don't break your other leg clomping out here to check up on us."

John chuckled. "You go on ahead," he said to Jonas and Phillip. "We old men will catch up with you. By the way, Doris Hooley is in the kitchen—she's fixed us a full dinner. I accompanied her to town this morning to purchase ingredients for the noon meal for the *leit* after church tomorrow, and she'll make those preparations here, too, so mind yourselves not to get in her way."

Doris was there again? Sawyer wondered how many times she'd visited that week.

His uncle interrupted his thoughts. "There's something I want to speak to you about. Something not usually discussed, but this isn't a usual situation. There's no easy way to say it, so I'll come right to the point—I'm courting Doris Hooley."

Sawyer puffed air out of his cheeks. Was John kidding him? Did Jonas set him up to say that as a prank?

"One of the reasons I'm telling you," his uncle continued, "is because she's bound to be here more frequently. Given our age and the fact that I'm not mobile enough to take the buggy to visit her—not to mention, we all benefit from her cooking—it seems easiest for her to come here. I wanted to be sure you're not uncomfortable with that. You understand no impropriety would ever occur between the two of us. I hold Doris's reputation in the highest regard."

"Of course." Sawyer was stumped and didn't know what else to say.

"I know I said she has the reputation of being *desperate*, but that's not how I see her, now that I've gotten to know her. She's made many sacrifices to help our family lately, especially given that the boys are not always receptive to her. *Jah*, she's a terrific cook and she dotes on me, but what I enjoy most is that I can talk to her about things. She offers a perspective only a woman can give. And she makes me laugh, which I haven't done for years."

"I see," said Sawyer, who understood too well what his uncle meant. "Then you have my blessing."

"Denki," John replied. "Now, at the risk of embarrassing you all the more, I'm going to give you a piece of advice."

"If the grass looks greener on the other side, fertilize?"

Sawyer joshed, growing uncomfortable with the direction of the conversation.

"Who told you that gem? Jonas?" John howled. "*Neh*, my advice is that you're too young to stay a widower for the rest of your life. You owe it to the *kinner*. Trust me, it only gets more difficult to raise them alone as they grow. But more than that, you owe it to yourself. There's no substitute for the kind of companionship—the kind of *love*—a woman and man share, especially a husband and wife. You know that."

Sawyer did know there was no substitute for that kind of love, which was exactly why he didn't expect he'd find anything quite like it ever again. But perhaps John was right. Perhaps it was time for him to consider marriage for the sake of the children. He couldn't expect Gertrude to live with them forever, and there was no denying how much healthier and happier they were with Hannah in their lives. Granted, he'd known her only a short while, but he and Hannah shared a growing affinity for one another. He wondered if, with more time, she might consider the possibility of an enduring relationship.

As they slowly made their way to the house, John seemed to read Sawyer's thoughts. "If you're considering courting someone, you should ask her soon," he suggested. "After all, you know what they say. 'One of these days is none of these days.'"

"That's interesting advice from someone who's moving so slowly he might as well be going backward," Sawyer joked.

"Hey!" John shouted, swinging his crutch. "I can't help it. I'm injured!"

But Sawyer had already bounded into the house, where Doris had lunch waiting for them.

* * *

"Now how are we going to make the pies?" Sarah howled when she realized the boys hadn't managed to salvage a single egg.

Hannah was less worried about the pies than she was about the fact she and her grandfather had only two chickens left to see them through the winter.

"We will borrow some from Grace Zook," she stated calmly. "Simon and Samuel, please run to their house and tell her I need six more eggs for pie crusts for church dinner tomorrow. Grace will be happy to share."

"But what if that fisher cat is lurking?" Simon asked.

"It isn't. *Groossdaadi* scared it off."

"What...what if it's hiding?" he persisted.

"It's not. Her *groossdaadi* killed it," Samuel answered knowledgeably. "With the ax he uses for chopping wood."

"Your *groossdaadi* killed a cat?" Sarah wailed, and a torrent of tears streamed from her eyes.

"Hush!" Hannah raised her voice and clapped her hands. "It was a weasel, not a cat, and *Groossdaadi* didn't kill it with an ax—he chased it away with a shovel. It's gone now, but if it makes you feel better, I will walk with you."

"Can we carry the shovel?" Simon inquired.

"It's '*may* we carry the shovel,'" Sarah corrected.

"Hush!" Samuel ordered her. "You're always doing that. You're not our teacher."

"Kinner!" Hannah exclaimed, exasperated. "I am going to the Zook house myself. Sarah, you are going to finish sweeping up the flour in the kitchen. Samuel and Simon, you are going to scrub the broken eggs from the porch and parlor. When I return, each of you is getting a bath."

Lord, give me patience, she prayed as she trudged through the field. Inhaling deeply, she mused that she suddenly had a new appreciation for her grandfather's mandate that "children should be seen, not heard." Her frustration was short-lived, however; when she spotted a hawk circling above, she wished the children were there to witness it with her, and she hurried home to tell them about it.

"Did her *hinkel* lay enough eggs?" Sarah asked anxiously.

"I don't know. She wasn't home," Hannah replied. "But don't worry—there's still plenty of time. We'll check back in a little while. *Kumme*, get the boys. You all may wash off in the stream. That's more fun than taking a bath any day. I'll carry a large walking stick so Simon doesn't fret about the fisher cat."

The air was so saturated with humidity that Hannah allowed the children to lollygag longer than usual in the water, so by the time they returned to the house, her grandfather was knocking around, grousing about how hungry he was.

She quickly browned half a dozen pork chops, placed them into a glass dish, covered them with onion, Worcestershire sauce and homemade cream of mushroom soup, and then slid them into the oven for baking. After eating, she and Sarah washed, wiped and put away the dishes while the boys helped her grandfather clean his workshop and stack the firewood he split for the autumn.

The third time they journeyed to the Zooks' farm and found no one there, they sat on the grass in the shade before making the trek back home.

Samuel suggested, "Couldn't we take the eggs from the coop and leave a note?"

"Of course not!" scolded Sarah. "That's stealing!"

"It is not!" Simon contradicted. "We'd leave a note. Besides, Hannah said Grace Zook would be happy to share. What do you think, Hannah?"

"I think the three of you have been clucking more than

the *hinkel* today!" Hannah laughed. "Come close, so I can give you a big hug beneath my wings."

She lifted her arms and they moved closer to snuggle, despite the heat. She squeezed them so awkwardly that they toppled over into a pile on the grass, laughing like mad. They lay there a long time, their heads touching, telling each other stories about the clouds, until Hannah abruptly sat up.

"Listen," she said. "Doesn't that sound like the Zooks' buggy coming down the lane?"

As drained as he was from laboring in the heat, Sawyer had a hunch Hannah was even more depleted. When he approached their home, he spotted the boys throwing a ball to each other on the grass. Sarah was slumped forlornly on the swing.

"Difficult day?" he questioned Hannah.

"Oh, she's upset because there was a mishap with the eggs," she explained. "We had to borrow from the neighbor, and by the time we had them in hand, it was too late to make the pies for church dinner tomorrow."

"Neh," Sawyer said. "I meant did *you* have a difficult day?"

"Me? Why do you ask?"

"For one thing, I could see from a mile away that Sarah was pouting, which is enough to try even the most patient person's nerves. And for another…" He hesitated. "Either you've gone gray in the past few hours or there was an explosion in your kitchen."

"Ach!" Hannah exclaimed, reaching to touch her hair. "It's flour. I called on Grace Zook looking like this, as well. She never mentioned it."

"She was probably too distracted by the grass," Sawyer joked, pulling a few blades from Hannah's tendrils.

She giggled so hard she started to cough. "I have to admit, we've had our challenges today."

"Did the *kinner* misbehave? I will speak to them if—"

"*Neh*, they were fine. It's nothing I couldn't handle. I think this oppressive humidity wears on us all, don't you?"

Sawyer wasn't convinced the weather was to blame for his children's behavior, but he had every confidence that if Hannah said she handled it, the issue was resolved.

"There is one thing I'd like your permission to do, however," she requested. "You know how eager Sarah was to help me bake pies for tomorrow's dinner, and you can see by how readily she just relinquished the swing to her brothers that she's thoroughly disappointed."

Sawyer glanced in the direction of the willow and nodded.

"Would you allow her to stay overnight with me? As soon as you boys skedaddle, she and I will get to work on the crusts. I won't let her stay up too late—I'll just let her complete the first few pies with me. She'll be a big help, and we'll bring her to the service with us in the morning."

"That's very kind of you," Sawyer acknowledged. "But we both know she'll be more of a hindrance than a help. And I don't want your *groossdaadi's* rest disturbed."

"My *groossdaadi* is a sound sleeper—he's deaf, remember?"

"You have so much baking to do before dawn. Sarah is the last person you need distracting you."

"On the contrary, teaching her will help me stay focused on what I'm doing. Please, Sawyer, for me?" she entreated, batting her eyelashes and clasping her hands in exaggerated petition. "Please?"

"How can I say *neh*?" he replied, reveling in their chitchat. “But remember, if you wind up wearing apple slices in your hair to church services tomorrow, I tried to warn you I thought Sarah would get in the way!”

Chapter Eleven

Sarah was so euphoric about being able to spend the evening helping Hannah and then sleeping at her home overnight that she chattered nonstop the entire time they were baking. Hannah didn't mind; it truly did keep her awake, and once they got a rhythm down of measuring, mashing and mixing, they turned into a two-*maedel* pie-making factory. Before long, the aroma of the first pies was emanating from the oven.

"With that fragrant smell in the house, we're all bound to have *sweet* dreams," Hannah punned as she tucked Sarah into bed in Eve's old room.

"The whole day was like a sweet dream," Sarah murmured, settling into her pillow and closing her eyes. "Especially this part, when I got to stay with you."

Hannah was tickled. Only a child who had gotten what she wanted most could ever call this day sweet! But Hannah felt the same way herself—for all of its chaos, she'd prefer this day of "nanny-hood" to the most serene day of solitude. Sarah's remark was so dear it kept Hannah energized as she continued to slide pies into and out of the oven until midnight, when the last one was completed.

In the morning, her grandfather didn't seem surprised to see Sarah at the breakfast table. "You two kept me awake last night with all that baking," he complained.

Hannah wondered how in the world he could make that

claim, but Sarah nodded her head knowingly and enunciated in her grandfather's direction. "Next time, we will make something that doesn't smell so loud."

To Hannah's surprise, her grandfather threw back his head and laughed. *"Denki,"* he said. "I'd appreciate that."

Because she would be helping Doris clean up and host until the last person left, Hannah had warned her grandfather she might not return home until evening. So, after preparing and setting aside his supper, she saw to Sarah's grooming. Then the three of them loaded the pies onto large pieces of wood and carried them like trays to the lane, where they waited for Doris to transport them to the Plank farm.

"Guder mariye, Daed," Sarah shouted happily when they arrived and she spied Sawyer hustling with his cousins in their direction. Doris disembarked, taking a board of pies from Hannah's grandfather, who agreed to hitch the buggy in the designated area once they'd unloaded it.

Sarah climbed down next, warning, "Jonas and Phillip, you may carry these but you can't taste them. Don't worry—Hannah and I made a secret extra pie for us to have after everyone else has gone."

"I think you just told the secret, Sarah," Sawyer chided as he helped Hannah with the last of the cargo. "But it looks like you and Hannah made plenty for everyone anyway. You must have been up half the night."

"Not at all," Hannah said as she handed him a pie. "We had a very sound sleep."

"You wouldn't tell me if you didn't, would you?" he teased.

"Are you saying I don't look rested?" she jested back.

"*Neh*, I've learned better than to suggest that!" Sawyer protested, adding, "Even if your hair *is* still coated in flour."

"It is not!" Hannah squealed.

"*Neh*, it's not, but even if it were, it wouldn't matter. *Gott* looks at the heart, not at outward appearances. And so do I," Sawyer said. Turning red, he stammered, "Which isn't to say you're not beautiful on the outside, because of course you are, with or without flour in your hair. What I mean is, it was a beautiful thing you did for Sarah. It meant so much to her. *Denki*."

"It meant so much to me, too," Hannah replied, and although Sawyer used his free arm to assist her down from the buggy, it felt as if her feet never touched the ground.

"Daed," Sarah whispered after the lunch dishes had been washed and put away and most of the *leit* had departed. "Hannah said I mustn't fish for compliments, but did you try the pie?"

"I thought it was so *gut* the first time, I tried it twice to make sure I wasn't mistaken," he replied, winking at her before she skipped away to find Abigail.

"What are you doing?" Jonas asked from behind. Phillip was with him.

"Setting up the volleyball net, in case the young people want to play."

"The *young people*," Jonas emphasized, "are leaving to socialize in another district. I'm letting Phillip tag along. We've finished the afternoon milking, so we'll see you later."

Jacob Stolzfus was twisting the other pole into the ground. "Aw, c'mon, almost everyone's gone home. You and Phillip can't leave now! Sawyer and I need at least two more players."

"I'll play," Doris announced from the porch.

"So will I," echoed Hannah.

"I don't suppose anyone would choose either of us to

be on their team, would they, Miriam?" John joked in reference to their physical conditions.

"I'm comfortable right here in this rocking chair," she claimed. "I'll keep score."

"Can we play?" Simon asked.

"*Jah*, can we? Can we?" begged Sarah, Samuel and Abigail.

"Sure," Sawyer agreed. "*Kinner* against adults."

"Daed!" they moaned, and Sawyer laughed. "Okay, okay, I pick Hannah for my team. And Abigail and Simon. Jacob, you get Doris, Sarah and Samuel."

"You had the opportunity to pick me and you passed it by?" Doris whined, insulted. "Except for you, I'm the tallest person here."

"Hannah may be tiny, but she's mighty," Sawyer replied with a laugh. "I'd choose her every time."

"Let's see what size of a portion you get the next time I make dinner here—it might be tiny, too!" Doris shot back, and everyone cracked up.

After an hour or so of a friendly tournament, Doris and Hannah served leftovers on the picnic table, and then Miriam, Jacob and Abigail said their goodbyes.

"It's almost dusk," Hannah said as she sipped a glass of water. "We should be going, too, Doris, shouldn't we? My *groossdaadi* might be wondering what's become of me."

"I thought you mentioned to him you'd be late?" Doris objected. "I promised the *kinner* we'd watch for shooting stars tonight, and it's not nearly dark enough yet."

Sawyer sensed that Doris's main objective was to stargaze with John, not with the *kinner*, but he decided to take her up on the offer.

"The *kinner* will appreciate that," he said. "Since Hannah is concerned about her *groossdaadi*, I will take her home now and return in time to put Sarah, Samuel and Simon to bed. *Denki*, Doris and John."

Hannah leaped to her feet. "I'll accompany you to hitch up the horses," she volunteered, and the two of them left before Doris could change her mind.

Dusk blended into night as they drove toward Hannah's house, and the darkness created a sense of cozy togetherness. Sawyer didn't speak until the horse stopped in Hannah's yard. There were no lamps glowing from the house.

"It looks like your *groossdaadi* is asleep."

"I think I worry about him worrying about me more than he actually worries," she said and gave a little giggle. "If that makes sense."

"Somehow, it does," Sawyer admitted, reluctant to move. He wanted to delay their parting for as long as he could.

"I should step down," she said.

"Please don't." The words were out of his mouth before he had time to temper the urgency with which he spoke them. "I mean, the boys told me about the fisher cat. Aren't they nocturnal?"

"Primarily, *jah*. Yet remember—I'm small but I'm mighty," she taunted. "You said so yourself."

"Actually, Simon and Samuel said so. They told me all about your ax-wielding abilities."

Hannah laughed. "Their stories are greatly exaggerated, I'm sure. What else did they say about me?"

"What *don't* they say? It's 'Hannah this' and 'Hannah that' all day long. I worry that when we return to Ohio, my poor sister Gertrude will feel put out by their praise of you."

"*Neh*, I hear plenty of *wunderbaar* stories about her, too," Hannah assured him. "Besides, it's not a competition. People care about one another in unique ways and there's room enough for all, especially when love is involved."

Although Hannah was speaking about loving the children, her words caused Sawyer to think of Eliza. Without knowing it, Hannah touched upon the conflict Sawyer felt about being drawn to her. He supposed she was right; people cared about each other in unique ways—their caring wasn't a competition. His interest in Hannah didn't negate the love he'd shared with Eliza, did it?

Hannah continued to speak hesitantly. "In fact, you might be surprised to find Gertrude was relieved that someone else assumed the primary maternal role in the *kinner's* lives for a season."

"What do you mean by that?" Sawyer asked.

"Oh, nothing," Hannah replied. "I've overstepped my bounds. I really should say *gute nacht* now."

As she hopped down from the buggy, she could hear Sawyer following close behind.

"Wait," he said, touching her elbow. "Please tell me what you meant by that. Are you tired of caring for the *kinner*?"

"Neh!" she objected. "Not at all. It's just that…"

She walked toward the swing and sat down before saying anything more. Sawyer played with the ropes overhead, causing her to twist back and forth.

"It's just what, Hannah? Please tell me."

"It's just I know what it's like to be responsible for raising *kinner* when you're barely out of childhood yourself."

"Ah," Sawyer said thoughtfully, letting go of the ropes.

"Please understand, I know that *Gott* calls us to serve one another—that our service to our families is part of how He provides for us. From what the *kinner* tell me, you and your wife served Gertrude by raising her when your *mamm* and *daed* died. She in turn served you and Samuel, Simon and Sarah by helping raise them when you lost your wife."

Sawyer nodded, so Hannah continued.

"I don't regret one instant of taking care of Eve when she was young. I'm honored the Lord gave me that privilege. But after *Groossmammi* died, there were times when I could have benefited from another adult giving me a hand. I do wish, when I was the proper age, I might have been afforded the opportunity to experience the pleasures of being a young adult."

Hannah had never confided these feelings to anyone, and she felt raw with vulnerability, waiting for Sawyer to respond.

His voice was throaty when he asked, "What pleasures do you mean?"

Hannah was glad it was too dark for Sawyer to see the tear trickle down her cheek. "Pleasures such as going to singings. Or walking out with a young man. I mean, there were a few suitors, but I didn't feel strongly enough about them to make it worth battling *Groossdaadi* for permission to be courted. Either that, or they didn't feel strongly enough about me to risk *Groossdaadi's* intimidation."

"I can't imagine that!" Sawyer declared. "Any suitor worth his weight would stop at nothing to walk out with such a fine young woman."

"Denki," Hannah said with a sigh. "But after enough refusals, they gave up on me and I gave up on my *groossdaadi's* behaviors. Time passes, just like that, so here I am, unmarried at twenty-nine."

Fearing she'd said too much, she forced a cheerful note into her voice. "I'm not complaining—if it weren't for my grandparents, especially *Groossdaadi*, who knows what would have become of Eve and me. Most people find him difficult, but I couldn't love my *groossdaadi* more than I do, and I consider it a privilege to care for him and contribute to our household. And although I don't have *bobblin* of my own, I've been blessed to teach the district's *kinner*. Of course, teaching isn't the same as motherhood—that's why it's been especially rewarding to care for Samuel, Simon and Sarah. I've gotten a little taste of what it's like to be a *mamm*."

"You're absolutely certain you're not tiring of it?"

"Of course not!" she insisted. "Now, do me a favor."

"What is it?"

"Give the swing a little push. Actually, give me one hundred pushes, please. That's Sarah's rule—one hundred pushes per turn per person."

"My daughter makes a lot of rules." Sawyer guffawed. He moved behind Hannah and gently lifted the swing, then set it in motion by releasing it. "And my sons *break* a lot of rules."

"You have very obedient, thoughtful, helpful *kinner*," Hannah said, stretching her legs toward the sky. It was as if her muscles remembered the movements from childhood, and she pumped harder to gain more height. "You're doing a fine job raising and instructing them."

"Sometimes I worry because they haven't a woman—an adult woman—present in the household. As you've pointed out, Gertrude is barely out of childhood herself. She is competent with their everyday care, but her judgment is… It hasn't reached its full maturity yet."

Hannah didn't want to pry, but since she had just divulged her innermost struggles to Sawyer, she felt comfortable asking him, under the cloak of night, "Yet, you've not remarried…?"

He stepped around from behind her and walked forward a few paces in silence, his back toward her as he searched the sky. She dragged her feet on the grass until she came to a stop. She was about to apologize for her trespass into such a personal subject when he spoke.

"I never found anyone I'd consider courting, much less marrying. Not in Blue Hill, anyway," he admitted, his voice hoarse. Suddenly, he pointed to the sky. "Did you see that? A shooting star!"

"I did!" Hannah exclaimed, springing from the swing to stand by his side. They allowed the silence to linger as they beheld the sky in awe.

"Well," Sawyer finally said. "I suppose Doris and the *kinner* saw it, too, so that means they can turn in for the night now. I should get back to put them to bed. Let me walk you to the door."

When they reached the porch, Hannah briskly climbed three stairs and then abruptly pivoted so she could be eye to eye with Sawyer, who hadn't begun to ascend them yet.

"As fond as I am of the *kinner*," she said, "I'm glad we had this opportunity to talk alone."

"I'm glad, too," Sawyer answered, his eyes shining in the moonlight. "In fact, you might say I planned it this way."

Overcome with a yearning to prolong the moment, Hannah reached forward and ever so tenderly traced the wound on his forehead. "It's getting better," she whispered before sliding her hand down along the side of his cheek.

Holding her gaze, he wrapped his fingers around her wrist and drew her hand to his mouth. He pressed his warm lips against her open palm once before agreeing, "Much better."

Then he turned on his heel and disappeared into the night.

As he unhitched his horse, Sawyer noticed Doris's buggy was gone. John was sitting alone on the porch when Sawyer got to the house. So much for their private stargazing.

"You're drinking coffee at this hour?" he asked his uncle, who lifted a cup to his lips.

"*Neh*, it's tea," John replied sheepishly. "Doris got me started on this."

"She's left already, I see. Did the *kinner* spoil your solitude?" Sawyer ribbed him.

"On the contrary, we *all* caught a glimpse of a falling star before Doris tucked them in and then left at a respectable hour," asserted John. "Speaking of solitude, you certainly ushered Hannah away from here quickly."

"She didn't want her *groossdaadi* to worry about her."

"Everyone around here knows her *groossdaadi* is a mean old coot. The only thing he worries about is what time his supper is going to be on the table."

"Nobody's all bad," Sawyer said softly. "I was sure grateful he was looking out for my sons when the fisher cat came around."

"Aha, I knew it!" John slapped his good knee. "A man defending Albert Lantz can only mean one thing—you're smitten with Hannah!"

Admitting to himself he had feelings for Hannah was one thing, but acknowledging it to John was quite another, so Sawyer replied, "Of course I'm fond of her. She's my *kinner's* hired nanny, and she provides them *wunderbaar* care," Sawyer replied.

"I'm not talking about your professional relationship, and you know it. Tell me your heart doesn't skip a beat every time she looks at you with those enormous baby blues," John pressed him.

Sawyer's voice cracked as he tried to deny it. "You're so taken with Doris you think everyone else is secretly courting each other, too."

"If you don't want to admit it, fine. I won't force you," John relented. "But mark my words—if you want to capture Hannah Lantz's heart, you better capture her *grooss-daadi's* first. She won't do anything without his approval."

"Jah, jah," Sawyer said, opening the screen door. "Enjoy your solitude, John. I'm going inside."

"I'm right. You'll see!" John called, chuckling.

Fifteen minutes later as he lay in bed, Sawyer contemplated how correct John was about Hannah's grandfather's possessiveness—she had told him as much herself. But that was years ago. People changed. Her grandfather couldn't possibly be that controlling now that she was an adult, could he?

As he rolled onto his side, the pillowcase fluttered against his cheek and he thought of Hannah's fingertips against his skin. Even if her grandfather was resistant to the idea of him courting Hannah at first, Sawyer decided he would win his favor. But how? Perhaps with a small gift, something that showed he was grateful to have both Hannah and her grandfather in his children's lives. He could imagine half a dozen presents suitable for Hannah, but not a single idea came to mind for her grandfather. Stumped, he closed his eyes and pictured shooting stars until he fell asleep.

Hannah willed herself to stay awake. She didn't want to slumber, lest at sunrise she should discover she'd dreamed the entire day, from the morning, when Sawyer referred to her as beautiful, inside and out, to the evening, when he kissed her hand—and all of the wonderful moments in between.

But when Monday dawned and Sawyer greeted her at school with a shy radiance about his face as he said, "It is a pleasure to see you, as always, Hannah," she knew her dream was a reality that wasn't about to vanish anytime soon.

Even the clammy weather couldn't dampen her spirits. "We should take a field trip to the stream tomorrow," she announced to her class. "We'll bring sketch pads and study the plant life we find there. We can dip our feet in the water as we're eating our lunches. I'll make a special apple dessert from a recipe my sister sent me. We'll have a celebration before harvest ends. How does that sound?"

"It sounds great!" Caleb acknowledged.

"Jah," the other scholars agreed.

"I think it sounds like a poor idea." Samuel pouted. "I don't want to go."

"But, Samuel, you love the stream," Hannah said.

"I used to, but I don't anymore," he argued. "I'm not going."

Hannah was stunned. Samuel had never talked back to her or refused to participate in a school activity. She quietly dismissed the rest of the scholars for lunch hour, asking Samuel to stay indoors so she could get to the bottom of what was troubling him.

"Samuel, please come to my desk," she requested, and he complied. "Now then, what happened to make you dislike the stream?"

His eyes welled with tears, but he chewed his lip and wouldn't speak.

"Are you frightened of the fisher cat?" she guessed. "Because I don't think he's around anymore. But we will say a prayer for safety before we leave, and I'll carry a big walking stick again, too."

Samuel hung his blond head, and his little shoulders heaved as he cried into his palms.

"Oh, Samuel," Hannah gasped. "When you're so sad, it makes me sad. Please tell me what's bothering you."

"The stream is our special place," he sobbed. "Now you're going to share it with everyone else."

"Oh," Hannah murmured. "And that makes you sad?"

"Jah," he hiccuped.

"But I've seen you share things with your sister and brother and classmates all the time. I thought you like to share."

"I do," Samuel replied, sobbing harder.

"Then why does sharing the stream make you cry?"

"Because pretty soon, I won't be here to share it."

"Oh, Samuel, that makes me very sad, too," Hannah whispered, fighting back tears herself as she enveloped the boy. "But I'm so greedy I want to have as many special days with you as I can before you leave. That way, when you are gone, I can go to the stream and think of you there and I won't be so lonely because I'll have a memory to call to mind."

Samuel's breathing slowed as Hannah patted his back. She continued, "If you don't want to come to the stream with your classmates, I understand. But I wish you'd come and help me make another memory. Not to mention, you know where all the best rocks are, so I was hoping you'd show the other scholars how to flip them over very carefully to see what's underneath."

"Jah," the boy agreed. He wiped his face with his sleeve and announced valiantly, "I'll carry the big walking stick for you, in case the fisher cat is still lurking. Because your hands will be full with the special apple dessert, right?"

"Right!" She laughed, tousling his hair. "Now scamper outside and tell your friends you changed your mind. They'll be glad to hear it."

After he left, she realized the half-truth of her advice to the boy. Yes, having memories to call to mind *could* help during times of separation—but sometimes the more memories people created together, the greater their loneliness became when they were apart.

As she blotted her desk where her own tears had fallen

and pooled, she prayed, *Please, Lord, provide us the comfort only You can provide.* She was going to need it.

It had taken considerable thought, but Sawyer finally drummed up a couple of gestures that he hoped would put Hannah's grandfather in a better frame of mind when Sawyer discussed his interest in Hannah with him. In conversing with Turner King after services on Sunday, Sawyer had learned about the expensive repairs Albert Lantz's buggy would require. He knew Hannah and her grandfather would be hard-pressed to afford them, so he decided to commission Turner to begin the necessary work.

In this regard, Sawyer's generosity was spurred not as much by an attempt to win the grandfather's favor, but rather by concern about Hannah's transportation, especially into town, or during inclement weather or emergencies. In fact, on Monday when he went to the repair shop, he made Turner promise not to tell Albert or Hannah—or anyone in the district—who paid for the repairs.

"I don't want you to lie, of course, but you can leave the details unsaid," Sawyer suggested. "For all anyone knows, you were compensated from the district's mutual aid fund."

Turner pledged to deliver the buggy to Albert first thing on Friday morning if Sawyer paid him on Thursday evening, which Sawyer promptly did. After stopping by Turner's shop with the payment, Sawyer was off to his second stop: the Hershbergers' farm, where he made a much smaller purchase—the gift he hoped would soften Albert up and show him Sawyer had his and Hannah's best intentions in mind.

His final destination was Hannah's house. Hopping from the buggy, he pulled the crate from the floor.

"*Daed*, *Daed*, what's in there?" the children asked as they charged across the grass.

"It's for Hannah."

Even from a distance, her smile caused his pulse to race.

"For me? What in the world—"

As he approached her, a fluttering of wings inside the crate gave away the surprise.

"Hinkel!" Simon pronounced.

"Hinkel?" Hannah repeated as Sawyer set the box at her feet.

"Four of them!" Sarah counted.

"To replace those that were, er, lost," Sawyer explained. Noticing Hannah's expression, he stated, "You're disappointed."

"Neh," she protested. "It's a very thoughtful gesture for you to have picked these up for us. But you must allow me to pay you for them."

"Of course not," Sawyer argued. "They're a gift."

The children had lifted the chickens from the crate and were following them around the yard as they pecked for bugs. Hannah's laughter sounded more nervous than amused, but Sawyer had no idea why.

"Hens aren't the kind of gift a man gives to a woman he fancies, are they?" he finally asked. "It's been so long, I've forgotten."

Hannah's eyes were even more captivating than her smile when she tipped her head and asked, "You *fancy* me, then, do you?"

"I thought that was obvious," he replied. "I actually feel as if we have been courting already. Not in the traditional sense of my taking you home after singings and such, but, you know..."

"*Jah*, I do know, and I agree," Hannah confirmed. "Despite bemoaning the fact I never had a real opportunity to go through the teenage rites of passage, I actually appreciate it that as adults, we can skip some of the awkward rituals, can't we? The hens were a lovely idea, but you needn't give me a gift."

"I wanted to," he insisted until he saw her face cloud over again. "But if you don't want them, I will take them away."

"I *do* want them. The *gut* Lord knows what it meant to us when we lost four at once. It's just that my *groossdaadi* is such a proud man. He would rather we go hungry than accept a gift."

"That's ridiculous!" Sawyer shouted, and then moderated the volume of his voice. "My *kinner* eat here every evening and all day on Saturday. It's the least I can do."

"Actually, that's not true," Hannah debated. "The least you can do is pay me, which you do handsomely. The hens are beyond generous. I wish I could accept them, but I don't want...I don't want my *groossdaadi* to lash out at you."

"I understand," Sawyer said, although he wasn't entirely sure that was true. How could Albert Lantz be such a stubborn man? It would be one thing if he was the only one who suffered for his pride, but he created hardship for Hannah, as well. "John will be glad to have an extra *hinkel* or two."

Hannah gave his hand a quick squeeze. "*Denki*, Sawyer," she whispered. "I appreciate all of the ways you've been considerate of me."

He felt anything but considerate toward Hannah's grandfather as he reclined in bed that evening. Sadly, he didn't think there was anything he could do to gain his favor. John may have been right after all; Hannah's grandfather was nothing but a mean old coot.

Chapter Twelve

"Yoo-hoo," Doris called, interrupting the coveted moments of conversation Hannah got to spend with Sawyer before the children trickled into the school yard. "What a gorgeous day, isn't it? There's finally a hint of autumn in the air."

"Jah," Hannah replied impatiently. "But I'm sure you're not interrupting us to discuss the weather."

Sawyer raised his eyebrows at her and stifled a laugh.

"Neh," Doris agreed obliviously. "I came to invite you both to visit on Sunday afternoon. I've invited John, as well. Miriam and Jacob won't be attending, as Miriam has to minimize her travel to the bare necessities. But Amelia and James will be home, of course, and we plan to serve a scrumptious supper."

"Denki," Hannah replied, chagrined that she'd been so dismissive of Doris. "I appreciate the offer, but as you know, my *groossdaadi's* buggy is in a state of disrepair, so..."

She let the thought dangle, hoping Sawyer would pick up on the hint.

"I will bring you," he immediately volunteered.

"Of course, the *kinner* and your *groossdaadi* are *wilkom* to attend, as well," Doris graciously offered.

"Actually," Sawyer said, "the boys have been invited

on a picnic with Caleb and Eli's family, and Sarah will be spending the afternoon at Abigail's house."

"I will invite *Groossdaadi*," Hannah said, adding, "if it's no trouble for Sawyer to pick him up, as well. But he may decline since you know he rarely goes on Sunday visits."

"Of course I will be glad to pick him up, as well," Sawyer said.

Hannah noticed a curious look on his face when he agreed, and she couldn't help but wonder if he was thinking the same thing, which was that she hoped he chose not to attend. She didn't mean to be unkind, but an afternoon spent with Sawyer and her friends would be an experience she'd treasure—especially riding to and fro alone with Sawyer. She wanted to soak in every last moment with him before harvest ended and he returned to Ohio.

Please, Lord, she prayed fervently, *let me go with Sawyer alone to Doris's house. But if it's Your will to have* Groossdaadi *accompany us, provide me the patience to* wilkom *him as graciously as You always* wilkom *each of us into Your presence.*

To her astonishment, that afternoon when she and the children arrived home after dallying at the stream, she found a note on the kitchen table. In her grandfather's lopsided penmanship, it said:

You should not have written Eve about the buggy repairs—Menno paid for them. Gone to Lancaster. Back on Monday in time for dinner.—Albert Lantz.

If it weren't for his impersonal signature and the implied directive to leave dinner prepared for him on Monday, Hannah might have taken the note to be a forgery. The timing was too good to be true!

"Do you want me to put the water on to boil for potatoes?" Sarah's question broke through Hannah's disbelief.

"*Jah*, please do."

Hannah never wrote to Eve about the buggy, so she doubted Menno had paid for the repairs. Her brother-in-law knew better than to do that. It was more likely Bishop Amos heard of their situation and the repairs were paid for from the mutual aid fund. Poor Eve. Their grandfather would show up unexpected and he'd be on a rampage. That was the last thing she and her baby needed right now.

Yet as Hannah sat wringing her hands over the note, she was overcome with a second realization: she would have the house to herself for the weekend! Not only would she be able to accept Doris's invitation without her grandfather accompanying her, but she decided she'd invite Sawyer to join her and the children for supper on Saturday, as well.

Humming, she rose to cut the potatoes Sarah had been peeling. *Thank You, Lord,* she prayed silently, *for Your most unusual provisions concerning the buggy repairs and my own wishes, selfish as they may have been. Please keep* Groossdaadi *and the cars around him safe. And please give Eve an extra measure of patience this weekend. She will need it.*

Sawyer felt a small pang of guilt as he polished off his second piece of chicken potpie. He hoped Hannah's grandfather believed Menno when Menno inevitably denied paying for the repairs. Sawyer hadn't meant to cause any conflict between them.

But as he surveyed the table, with Hannah blotting her delicate lips with a napkin across from him, and his children hungrily finishing their robust portions, he had to admit to himself, he wasn't sorry that his actions resulted in Albert's absence.

"You're smiling, *Daed*," Sarah noticed. "That must mean you like the potpie I made with help from Hannah."

"What did she tell us about fishing for compliments?" Simon scolded. "Remember? We're supposed to take satisfaction in serving others and not point out our own *gut* deeds."

"Jah," Samuel agreed. "It's like when Hannah serves the apple goodie for dessert. Simon and I aren't supposed to boast about how hard we searched to find the ripest apples without any wormholes."

Sawyer caught Hannah's eye and winked. "At the risk of drawing attention to anyone's *gut* deeds, I will tell you that *was* a delicious potpie, Sarah. Now, let's see if there are any worms in the apple goodie, shall we?"

"Then may we go to the stream?" Samuel asked.

"I don't know if there will be time before dark," Hannah replied. "The days are getting shorter."

"But *Daed* is here. He'll protect us," Simon suggested.

"Please?" Sarah echoed.

"*Jah*, I'll protect you," Sawyer repeated. "Please?"

"I know when I'm outnumbered." Hannah giggled. "Alright, then, leave your dishes on the table and let's go now before the bats come out."

But by the time they got to the stream, the sun was on the verge of setting, so Sawyer forbade them to go wading. "We ought to get back to the farm. You're visiting your friends after we have our home church services tomorrow. You need a *gut* sleep."

"I wish we could stay overnight here," Simon hinted.

"Jah," agreed Samuel. "Sarah was allowed to stay overnight, but we didn't get a turn."

"You did, too!" Sarah protested. "Don't you remember?"

"We were sick. That doesn't count," Simon said. "You got a turn when you were sick and another when you were well."

"Stop your squabbling," Sawyer chided them. "You are not staying overnight."

Samuel suggested, "You could stay, too, *Daed.* You could sleep in Hannah's *groossdaadi's* bed."

"Then we could have breakfast and our family church worship time together here, since we're sort of a family," Simon proposed.

"Jah," Sarah agreed. "Hannah's our sort-of *mamm.*"

"*Gott* must love us a lot to give us our *mamm* and also a sort-of *mamm* like Hannah once our *mamm* died," Samuel reflected. "Doesn't He, *Daed*?"

Sawyer was startled by the insightfulness of his son's remark, which showed that while he'd never forget his mother, his heart was open to loving Hannah, too. Samuel's words caused Sawyer to remember Hannah saying when love was involved, it wasn't a competition—there was room enough for all. It was growing clearer to him that a space was expanding in his own heart, too.

"*Gott's* love and provisions for us are abundant, indeed," Sawyer resolutely confirmed. "But you heard my answer. We are not staying here overnight. Now run up ahead before I tickle the silliness right out of you."

Beneath pastel pink and vibrant orange clouds, the children bounded up the hill. Sawyer glanced sideways at Hannah and noticed she was biting her lip.

"I'm sorry if anything the *kinner* said embarrassed or… or bothered you," he stammered. "Despite your best efforts to teach them modesty and discretion, I'm afraid they still tend to say whatever they feel."

"A little candor can be refreshing," Hannah replied. "Especially when it comes from the mouths of babes. I fear it's *you* who was bothered by their remarks."

"On the contrary," Sawyer stated. His knees went weak as he gazed into Hannah's eyes. He dearly wanted to kiss her rosy pink lips, but he was afraid if he moved, he'd scare her off, like a bird.

"A bat!" Sarah shouted from the hilltop.

"It is not—it's a sparrow," Samuel argued back, just as loudly.

"*Neh*, it's an owl!" claimed Simon.

"Are you certain you don't want to keep my bickering brood overnight? They're yours for the taking," Sawyer joked, and he and Hannah laughed breathlessly all the way up the hill.

Hannah didn't mind washing the dishes on her own; it gave her something to do while she daydreamed. She felt guilty, knowing her pleasure was coming at such a cost to her sister, and she could only imagine the scenario that must have been unfolding at her home. But Eve got to experience married life alone with her husband daily. She had only the tiniest glimpse of that for one weekend, and as Simon would have said, it was her turn!

She didn't know what warmed her heart more: Sarah claiming, *Hannah's our sort-of* mamm, or the look Sawyer gave her when he denied being embarrassed by the sentiment. She fell asleep replaying every aspect of the evening in her mind, as clearly as if she were watching the scene take place with figures in the dollhouse her grandfather made.

Come morning, she was surprised by the slight chill in the air, and she thought to warn her grandfather to wear long sleeves. Then she remembered he wasn't home. She read Scripture and spent time in quiet prayer before fixing a second cup of tea. She'd never noticed how quiet it was there before. As the rocking chair creaked back and forth, she contemplated whether this was what it felt like for her grandfather to be deaf.

She was ready and waiting when Sawyer arrived at three

thirty. Before she could cross the lawn, he had stepped down and was heaving a potted plant from the buggy. Its lavender spray was so wide it nearly eclipsed his face as he ambled toward her.

"Russian sage!" she exclaimed. "And it's already in bloom for autumn."

"It's a perennial, you know," he said awkwardly and set it down on the porch. Then he glanced at it and back at her. "I was right. It reminds me of the color of your eyes."

If the three children weren't watching from the buggy, Hannah might have embraced him and never let go.

"Denki," she said. "It's lovely."

The children prattled about the day's upcoming events as they journeyed, much to Hannah's amusement. Sawyer dropped them off at their respective locations with warnings to mind their manners and a reminder that he'd be back after supper time but before dark to pick them up.

"After all, it's a school night," Sawyer joked as he and Hannah traveled alone down the lane. "I've heard their teacher is very strict."

"Oh, *neh*!" Hannah bantered back. "That's the *other* schoolteacher you must be thinking of. I'm the sweet one. I even have thimble cookies to prove it," she said, holding up the container she'd been carrying on her lap.

When Sawyer laughed, Hannah wished she could bottle the sound, so she could loosen the lid and listen to it anytime she wanted—especially after he returned to Ohio. She pushed the dreaded thought of his departure to the back of her mind.

"Why did you sigh just now? Did you forget something?" he asked as they pulled into Doris's lane.

"Neh," she answered. To herself, she thought, *I'm memorizing every part of this by heart.*

"Wilkom!" Doris called, flapping her hand. *"Kumme* around to the side. We're playing lawn croquet."

Hannah waited for Sawyer to unhitch the horse so they could join the group together. Amelia and Doris were settled into lawn chairs, but James and John were taking practice shots knocking the croquet balls through the hoops.

"John!" Hannah exclaimed. "Doris and Sawyer didn't tell me you got your cast off! When did that happen?"

The men stopped playing, and John limped over to where Hannah was standing with Sawyer. "I just got it off on Friday. The *Englisch* doc was surprised it had healed so nicely. He said most Amish men try to put too much weight on it too soon and it ends up needing to stay in the cast longer than not."

"So essentially what you're telling us is that you're lazier than most Amish men?" Sawyer joshed.

"Neh," John replied and took a friendly swing at him. He teetered on his good leg, and Doris jumped up to offer her arm to steady him. "What I'm telling you is that I couldn't have healed so quickly if it weren't for this lovely woman here."

For the first time in all of the years she'd known her, Hannah observed Doris blushing shyly and averting her eyes.

"*Denki*, John," she said demurely.

"In fact—" John cleared his throat "—it's no secret, since you've all been told by either Doris or me, that we've been courting. But what no one here knows—well, no one except for James, because I spoke to him about it before making it official—is that Doris and I are getting married."

By now, Doris was beaming, her head held high. "It's being published soon in church—even though John has been married already, I still want to follow the tradition of announcing it as a first-time bride. John told his sons last night, and we've already begun our meetings with the deacon. But other than those people—and now you—no one else knows. So please don't tell them."

"Who is there left to tell?" Sawyer quipped, and everyone laughed good-naturedly.

"That is *wunderbaar* news," Hannah managed to say. "When do you intend to hold your wedding?"

"The first Tuesday in November," Doris chirped.

"So soon?" Amelia questioned.

"It can't be soon enough for us," John said. "Doris has waited her entire life to marry. It's been five years since I buried my wife. We are past our youth, and we believe we're acting in wisdom, in accordance with the blessing *Gott* has provided us."

"The wedding day can't come quickly enough," agreed Doris. "There is only one obstacle we hope you will help us with, which is partly why we're confiding in you."

"What's that?" Amelia asked.

"We didn't have time in advance to plant an extra celery patch, and I don't need to point out how important celery is to the wedding meal!"

"I will save you every last stalk from my garden," Hannah pledged, before giving her friend a hug. "You'll have a surplus of creamed celery to share with your wedding guests and plenty left over to decorate the tables beside."

While the women were cleaning the supper dishes and James went to milk the cows, John said to Sawyer, "You know, the doc said I'll be up to speed in a week. Maybe not one hundred percent, but enough that the boys and I can manage what's left of harvesting by then."

Although he'd been champing at the bit to return to Ohio to sort out the problems at his shop, Sawyer suddenly found himself wishing he had more time in Willow

Creek. His mind reeled with the discussions he needed to have and the arrangements he needed to make with Hannah before he left.

But he said, "I'll help out through Saturday, then. We'll spend the Sabbath resting and leave first thing on Monday morning."

"I can't thank you enough." John choked out the words, his tone unusually serious.

"Nothing you wouldn't do—nothing you *haven't done*—for me," Sawyer said.

"Even so, it's humbling to have another man do your work for you. But Doris kept reminding me what a sin it is to be prideful and to refuse help from others. I'm indebted."

"You're not indebted—you're family."

The moment the last supper dish was done, Sawyer suggested that he and Hannah should leave in order to round up the children.

"Is it that time already?" Hannah's brow was furrowed, as if in disappointment.

"I don't want them to wear out their *wilkom*," he stated definitively.

After bidding their good-nights, they rode in silence before Sawyer pulled down a dirt lane.

"The Stolzfuses' house isn't this way," Hannah said, "although I can see why you'd be confused. That fence looks similar."

"I'm not confused. I turned here on purpose," he admitted, bringing the horse to a halt at the crest of the road, which opened to a magnificent field alive with birdsong and overrun with late-blooming wildflowers. "I wanted to spend a few moments with you alone, if that's alright."

"It is," she said, and they got out and ambled over to the fence.

Sawyer sat on the railing so his face was level with hers. Hannah's profile glinted with the light of the sun hanging low in the sky as she looked out over the field.

"Some of the leaves are beginning to change," she observed about a stand of trees in the distance.

"Jah," Sawyer agreed, briefly glancing over his shoulder in the direction she was pointing, but he only had eyes for her.

He pulled a tall piece of grass and used the tip of it to tickle Hannah's ear, causing her to giggle and swat it away. When she did, he clasped her hand, caressing her silky skin with his thumb as he spoke.

"So, you knew about John and Doris courting, too?"

"I did," she said. "Although the wedding news is a big surprise."

"Do you think it's too soon?" Sawyer had to know.

"Ordinarily, I might say *jah*, but John made a *gut* case for their getting married sooner rather than later. They are of a mature age, they're like-minded in important matters, such as family and beliefs, and they genuinely care for one another. But even if all that weren't true, who am I to judge what the Lord provides for someone else?"

Sawyer felt his mouth go dry, and he wiped the corner of his lips. "I agree," he concluded solemnly. "I couldn't have said it better myself."

She gave his hand a little tug before mentioning, "We should go. It's getting late."

But it's not too *late*, he said to himself, his thoughts elsewhere. Now that he had confirmed Hannah wasn't opposed to a brief courtship, he felt encouraged about asking her to become his wife. But first, knowing Hannah wouldn't leave her grandfather, Sawyer needed to come up with a plan to convince him the move to Ohio would benefit him, too. He mulled over his options as they journeyed to gather the children.

"How were your visits?" he asked them.

"We had a *wunderbaar* time with our friends," Samuel said, and Simon agreed.

"I had a *wunderbaar* time with my friend, too," Sarah claimed.

"How about that—so did I!" Sawyer trumpeted.

"Me, too," Hannah stated, giving Sawyer a gentle nudge. "I'm glad the Lord provided us all with such special friends."

"I'll see you bright and early tomorrow morning, *Gott* willing," Hannah called from the porch as the buggy pulled away.

Before she crossed the threshold to the house, she sensed something was different, the same way she could perceive when a storm was about to break. *My* groossdaadi *is back*, she thought.

Sure enough, a voice from the dim parlor yapped, "While you've been gallivanting who knows where, I've been sitting here hungry. After such a long trip, this is the *wilkom* I receive in my own home?"

Hannah turned on the gas lamp and faced him directly. She knew it was futile to remind him he wasn't expected until Monday, and she doubted Eve would have sent him off without enough food to feed him for a week.

"I'm sorry. I was visiting Doris Hooley. I will prepare your supper now."

"And ruin my sleep by eating so late?" he grumbled. "*Neh*, don't bother. I am going to bed."

Hannah bit her lip, but the tears came anyway. Try as she did to hold on to every good memory of the blessed weekend she had just experienced, she was crushed by the reality that it was undeniably over. Soon her relationship with

Sawyer and the children would be over, too, now that John's leg had healed and he no longer needed Sawyer's help. She thought she'd be content to experience just a fraction of what it would be like to be married with children—but instead, it had made her all the more aware of how wonderful it was. It had increased her longing tenfold.

She sat on the sofa a long while, sobbing into her arm, and she might have spent the night like that, were it not for a brilliant flash of lightning illuminating the window beside her. She leaped to her feet and moved to sit in her grandfather's chair beneath the lamp. She hadn't noticed it before, but he must have placed an envelope on the end table. *Hannah*, it was labeled in Eve's flowery penmanship. Sniffling, she tore it open.

"Dearest Hannah," it began. "Aren't the rocking chair, chest of drawers and cradle Grandfather made for us a most handsome set? We are so grateful."

Hannah was surprised. She knew her grandfather had spent an unusually long time working on the Stolzfuses' furniture, but she had no idea he was really working on an additional set. He must have been paying attention to her during mealtimes when she told him about Eve being with child after all. She read on:

> What a surprise it was to have Grandfather show up here unannounced, ranting about Menno paying for his buggy repairs. It took some convincing before he believed we didn't know anything about the matter, and we imagine the church was responsible for this generous act of charity. (Had we known, we would have contributed; in the future, you must share your struggles with us. We will find a way to help that doesn't offend Grandfather's sense of responsibility.)
>
> Despite his antics, I was—and I write this sin-

cerely—very glad to see him, because I've missed him in his own way, although I would have been much gladder if you had been present, as well. You see, while I've written that there is nothing like the bond between a mother and child, or between a husband and wife, there's also nothing like the love between sisters.

As your sister, in response to what you wrote in your last letter, please allow me to express my advice and my hopes for you. By now, your Sawyer Plank may have made—*should* have made—his intentions toward you clear. When a man is interested in a woman, there should be no guessing. His actions and his words should unequivocally reflect the intentions of his heart. There should be no guessing, no interpreting, no doubting how he considers you. It should be clear in everything he does and says. (Likewise, the same is true of a woman's consideration for a man.)

If that is the case with Sawyer, then I will pray God will somehow work a way to allow you more than just a "brief season" of sharing your mutual love. I want this for you as much as you want it for yourself, dear sister.

Your loving Eve

Hannah was really bawling now, but her tears were… not joyful, exactly, but hopeful. She hoped to marry Sawyer more than she'd ever hoped for anything in her life, and she decided if he asked her to become his wife, she'd agree, no matter what her grandfather wanted. She'd do everything she could to persuade him to accompany her, but if he refused, that was his decision to make, not her fault to bear.

A dull roll of thunder sounded in the distance as she climbed the stairs. *Lord,* she prayed beside her bed, *thank You for my sister, Eve. Please keep her and the* bobbel *healthy. Thank You for bringing* Groossdaadi *home safely. And if there is any possible way Sawyer and I might share a future together, please move Heaven and earth so it may come to pass.*

After he'd tucked the children into bed, Sawyer scribbled a quick letter to Gertrude:

Dear Gertrude,

I trust this letter finds you and Kathryn's household healthy? I especially pray for the strength and size of the baby.

We're grateful the Lord has healed John's leg, and the children and I will return to Ohio on Monday, God willing.

A little birdie told me a young suitor named Seth might have captured your attention, which is certainly understandable at your age, but I hope he will not keep you from returning to Blue Hill soon? The children have much to tell you, and so do I. (I hope there will be surprising new developments to report.)

Remember me to Kathryn and her family.

Your brother, Sawyer

After he sealed the note into an envelope, Sawyer turned in to his room for the night. Kneeling beside his bed, he prayed, *Lord, You have indeed given me someone very special in Hannah, just as you did with Eliza. Now I ask that Hannah's* groossdaadi *will be willing to allow her to marry me. And I ask for Your guidance in knowing how to approach him about it so the move is acceptable to him.*

As he turned down the lamp, Sawyer imagined the *daadi haus* he owned. Not much smaller than Albert's own home, it would offer Albert all the privacy and independence he wanted, yet would still allow Sawyer and Hannah to check in on him as needed. But, although older Amish in-laws frequently lived in such houses, Sawyer knew Albert would see it as charity. That man had no sense of humility or gratitude.

Sawyer punched his pillow and suddenly recalled John's words: *it's humbling to have another man do your work for you*. Perhaps that was how Hannah's grandfather felt. Didn't he say his affections couldn't be bought? It dawned on Sawyer that he shouldn't have tried to give him gifts. He should have valued the contributions Albert could make.

He immediately knew what the solution to his dilemma was: he would ask Albert to work in his shop. The man's hearing was gone, but his craftsmanship was still keener than most, and Sawyer desperately needed the help. He felt convinced that once her grandfather had a stake in moving to Ohio, nothing would stand in the way of Sawyer and Hannah becoming husband and wife.

Chapter Thirteen

Hannah woke early to prepare her grandfather a bigger breakfast than usual.

"I found Eve's letter," she mouthed. "She was very pleased with the furniture."

"Bah," he muttered, and she dared not ask him any other questions about his visit. For now, there was no need to say anything about the buggy repairs, either.

"That storm cooled things off last night, but it's shaping up to be hot again," she said, but he wasn't watching her lips, so she gave up conversing with him and set about making his dinner instead.

"Your eyes are…overcast," Sawyer stated when he greeted her in her classroom. "Did the storm keep you up last night?"

"*Jah.* We're probably in for some more tonight. The incoming autumn air makes for an unstable atmosphere."

"I couldn't sleep for imagining you last night, all alone," Sawyer said. Almost immediately, he turned a deep shade of crimson. "I mean, because I know how electrical storms rattle you so. At least tonight your *groossdaadi* will be home."

"Actually, he is already home. I was surprised to find he'd arrived while I was out visiting."

"Oh," Sawyer said somberly. "Did he confirm that Menno paid for his buggy repairs?"

Hannah giggled. "*Neh*, but according to a letter my sister, Eve, sent me, he must have put on quite a display interrogating them. They finally persuaded him they knew nothing about it."

"I see. So, is he well rested from his journey?"

"*Jah*, but why would you ask abo—"

"I knew I could find you here," Doris announced. "The two of you are always clucking away like hens. If I didn't know better, I'd think it was *you* who were betrothed!"

Hannah noticed Sawyer's jaw tense.

"What may we do for you?" she asked impatiently.

"I wanted to inquire if Sawyer will be bringing his younger sister to the wedding as well as the *kinner*. I heard from John she might still be in Indiana. My understanding is your eldest sister and her family most likely won't be able to attend, due to her weakened condition?"

Sawyer rubbed his forehead as if he had a headache. "I'm not certain, Doris," he said with a sigh. "Can't the answer wait a bit? We'll be heading home in a week and I can send John a letter once I've assessed the situation then, okay?"

"Of course," Doris gushed. "I only want them to know they're all invited."

"You're leaving in a week?" Hannah repeated, her heart pounding in her ears. "I knew John's leg had healed, but I thought you'd at least stay through the end of harvest."

"I was going to talk privately to you about that," Sawyer murmured quietly. Then, glancing at Doris, who was still hovering within earshot, he quickly added, "Because I wanted to prepare the *kinner* to say their farewells."

Hannah's mind whirled. Sawyer was leaving, just like that, as if their time together—especially these last few days—had meant nothing to him. And all he cared about was how his children felt about saying goodbye to her as their nanny, not how he felt about their parting. Not how *she* felt about it. She'd thought he valued the confidences they shared. She'd believed he saw her as strong and beautiful. That he considered her special as a woman—as "every bit a woman." The way he held her hand...the way he *kissed* her hand...the way he asked her opinion about Doris and John getting married so soon... She thought it was all leading up to one thing. What else was she to think?

Hannah recalled what Eve had written in her letter about how a man's actions and words should unequivocally reflect the intentions of his heart. Until that moment, Hannah had believed that everything Sawyer said, no matter how awkwardly it may have been expressed, reflected his true intentions. But his actions showed her where his heart was: in Blue Hill, Ohio. Now that the opportunity presented itself, he couldn't say his goodbyes quickly enough.

"Excuse me," someone said from the doorway. "May I speak with Hannah?"

"Jacob," Hannah acknowledged. "I'm sorry, but school is about to begin and I need a moment to prepare. If you're here about the arrangement we discussed, I'd be pleased to care for your household when my teaching assignment ends."

"*Denki*, Hannah," Jacob replied. "Miriam will be thrilled to hear this news, and so will Abigail."

"It's my pleasure. Now, everyone, please scoot. I have sums to prepare."

She turned her back before her eyes overflowed with the tears that had been gathering there.

Sawyer snapped the reins, and the horse took off. Hannah's disappointment was nearly tangible. He hadn't meant to spill the news he was leaving like that. His intention was to propose to Hannah once he'd spoken to her grandfather. Then they could work out the details together concerning the wedding and relocating. He didn't think about what he'd said before he said it—he just wanted to give a quick answer so Doris would leave. If she weren't always butting in, this never would have happened.

He had hoped to wait until Hannah's grandfather was rested from his trip and in a fairly reasonable mood. But now, as the horse trotted along, Sawyer realized he had to act with extreme urgency, and he redirected the animal toward Hannah's home.

He expected to find Albert in his workshop, and he tried to think of how he could enter without startling him. But when he arrived, Hannah's grandfather was sitting on the top step of the porch, sipping coffee as if he'd been expecting Sawyer all along.

"Guder mariye," Sawyer said when he positioned himself at the bottom landing, where his mouth was nearly at the same height as Albert's eyes.

The grandfather nodded but didn't reply.

"I'll be brief," he mouthed carefully. "I want to marry Hannah."

No sooner had the words left his mouth than the old man shook his head.

"Neh," he uttered. *"Neh."*

Sawyer wasn't dissuaded. "I want her to move to Ohio with me. I want you to come, too. I have a *daadi haus* for you to live in. I need another man in my shop. It isn't charity—I've seen your work. I need someone like you on my crew."

"This is my home. *That* is my shop." The man gestured, shouting. "Hannah is *my* granddaughter."

"I care for Hannah and so do my *kinner*," Sawyer

shouted back. He wanted the grandfather to see the intensity in his features, even if he couldn't hear it in the volume of his voice. "I want to be her husband and for her to be my wife."

"*Neh*, never!" her grandfather cried.

Sawyer's expression crumbled, but if there was one thing he resolved, it was that he wouldn't break down in front of Albert Lantz.

"But why not?" he questioned. "Why not?"

The grandfather stood and tossed the remains of his coffee cup onto the potted Russian sage, the hot spray narrowly missing Sawyer's shoulder.

"Never," he repeated evenly and then shuffled into the house, letting the screen door slam behind him.

"Ach!" Sawyer yelled and punched at the air.

When that did nothing to defuse his ire, he kicked the railing. To his astonishment, it splintered and cracked like a toothpick from the force of his fury, dangling crookedly from the side of the porch.

That is how you have trampled my heart, Albert Lantz, he thought as he sped away.

"You're later than usual," Jonas remarked when he strode into the barn a few minutes later. "And you look like a raging bull."

"Don't start with me," Sawyer warned. "I need your toolbox. I'll be back in the fields whenever I get there."

When he returned to Hannah's home, her grandfather was already beginning to repair the damage he had done.

Although the words were bitter on his tongue, he mouthed, "I'm sorry."

The old man nodded and they worked together on the repairs. As Sawyer had already observed from the toys Albert created, he was a skilled carpenter, and the finished result was so seamless, one might have never guessed it had been broken.

"Albert, please," Sawyer started to say.

"Never means never," the grandfather replied, and Sawyer knew he meant it, just as definitively as he'd meant it about never doing business with the Schrock family.

Sawyer took hold of his sleeve to get his attention. "Listen, this isn't about marrying Hannah. It's about the toys you made. I want to buy them. All of them."

He would resell them in Ohio. Meanwhile, as he journeyed toward the farm with the dollhouse in the second seat and a box of trains beside him, he took small consolation in knowing the money he paid for the toys would help see Hannah and her grandfather through a few months this winter, God willing.

"You look awful," Doris commented at lunchtime. "Are you ill?"

"I feel awful," Hannah said. Her stomach was doing flips and her head was buzzing, but it was the cavernous ache in her heart that hurt more than anything. She couldn't bear the thought of facing Sawyer that evening. "I am afraid I need to go home. Would you mind taking over my class and watching the Plank *kinner* after school?"

"Of course not. It gives me another opportunity to see my betrothed!"

Hannah managed to slip away before Doris could see that her words triggered a torrent of tears. She numbly marched along the meadow route home, crossing the stream without stopping to dip her feet. Although it was a muggy afternoon, she felt chilled to the bone. Ascending the incline behind the house, she decided to stop at her grandfather's workshop to let him know she was home early, but that she intended to nap before preparing supper.

She slowly pushed open the door so as not to startle him, but as her eyes adjusted to the light, she realized he wasn't inside. The fragrance of the wood shavings filled her nostrils, reminding her of the evening she ducked inside the workshop with Sawyer and the children. She shut her eyes and recalled his hands moving over her ankle as he gingerly examined it for an injury. She shuddered and pushed the memory from her mind.

Spotting the rocking chair her grandfather was working on for Miriam, she traced the smooth curve of the wood along the arm. On the floor beside it was a matching cradle. But something was missing. Something wasn't—

Scanning the room, she realized there were no toys on the shelves. The dollhouse was gone, as well. Did her grandfather take them to sell in Lancaster? It would have been unlikely, but she supposed it was possible.

Inside the house, she found him sitting at the kitchen table, finishing the dinner she'd prepared for him.

Before he could make a single demand of her, she put both hands on his shoulders and mouthed, "What have you done with the toys?"

"I sold them to Sawyer Plank."

"All of them?" she questioned incredulously.

"Including the dollhouse. His *kinner* are spoiled, are they not?"

"I'm ill and I'm going to bed," she responded and fled the room.

She barely unlaced her shoes before collapsing into bed. She wondered why in the world Sawyer wanted all of those toys. Were they really for his children? She didn't think he was the kind of father to lavish material goods on them, but what did she really know of his character? Until that morning, she actually thought he had intentions of asking her to marry him.

What a fool I've been! She wept into her pillow. She thought she was more than a nanny to his children, and more than a trifling flirtation to him. How could she have been so wrong? She'd finally allowed herself to believe that it wasn't too late and she might actually receive her heart's deepest desire. She'd finally allowed herself to *admit* her heart's deepest desire. Come to find out, she wasn't anywhere close to having what she so desperately yearned for.

"Is one weekend of bliss all I get?" she shouted in frustration. "It isn't fair. It just isn't fair!"

She slept through the afternoon and evening. When she felt a hand on her shoulder the next day, she pushed her grandfather's arm away. She didn't care about teaching now. She didn't care about watching the Plank children. She just wanted to sleep. Rather, she only wanted someone to rouse her from sleep to tell her this had all been a bad dream.

"I will make your breakfast in an hour," she said when her grandfather returned a second time. "I need more rest. I'm sick."

"I brought you eggs," he said and set a plate on the nightstand before leaving the room.

Hannah shifted to a sitting position. Her grandfather usually did kind things like that only when he felt guilty, but she was hungry enough not to care what had panged his conscience. She ate the eggs and half of the piece of burned toast and then got dressed.

The clock said ten thirty; plenty of time to get to school and relieve Doris from the burden of teaching her class a second day. No matter how despondent she felt, she had a responsibility to her scholars, and once her class ended, she would regret missing any time with them.

"I can feel the sun beating down on my skull right through my hair," she said when she saw her grandfather on the porch. He was sanding the railings, but she didn't question him about it. "I'm taking the shortcut to school. I feel better now—I think the eggs helped. *Denki.*"

"I will see you tonight, *Gott* willing." He continued scratching the wood smooth.

Hannah grew so sweaty on her way that when she arrived at the stream, she removed her socks and shoes to maneuver through the deepest water instead of using the stepping-stones. She had reached the opposite embankment when a man's voice called, "Hannah, wait!"

Hannah's expression was even icier than the water he was slogging through, but neither stopped Sawyer from rushing to her side.

"What are you doing here?" she asked, bending to lace her shoes.

"I was waiting for you. I had a hunch you might come here at some point."

"And if I hadn't?"

"Then I would have come back each day until you did," Sawyer exclaimed. "Listen, Hannah, I need to talk to you. It seems you're angry, and I can't return to Ohio knowing you're upset with me. Are you?"

"Did you buy my *groossdaadi's* toys for your *kinner*?" she asked, avoiding his question.

"Er, *jah*," Sawyer stammered. "I mean, *neh*."

"Which is it?" she asked, shooting him a penetrating look. "*Jah* or *neh*?"

"I bought the toys," he admitted loudly. "But not for my *kinner*."

"Then why?" she asked, standing akimbo. When he didn't answer, she threw her hands in the air and began stamping through the grass.

"Wait!" he called, hobbling barefoot after her, his shoes

and socks bundled in his arms. "I bought them to resell in Ohio. They'll garner a high price there, and I wanted you and your *groossdaadi* to have enough income to see you through the winter."

She whipped around and shrieked, "Your financial responsibility toward me ends when I stop caring for the *kinner* and you return to Ohio."

"You are as prideful as your *groossdaadi*, Hannah Lantz!" Sawyer hollered back as he tossed his footwear beside him. "I didn't purchase the toys out of responsibility or obligation. I purchased them because I care about you."

"You care about me? You care about me?" Hannah sobbed. "Not like I care about you, Sawyer Plank. I thought… I actually thought—"

"You thought what?"

"I thought you might be the Lord's intended for me." She wept, falling to her knees and burying her head in her hands.

"Oh, Hannah," Sawyer murmured, crouching down beside her. "I wanted to marry you, too. I had it all planned. I offered your *groossdaadi* employment in my shop. I told him I have a *daadi haus* he can occupy. I pleaded with him, but still he refused."

"Why?" she asked, intensely scrutinizing his face. Her eyelashes were damp with tears as she asked again, "Why?"

"I don't know," Sawyer moaned. "He wouldn't say."

"I mean why did you want to marry me?"

"What kind of question is that?"

"A direct one. Why won't you give a direct reply?"

"You already know why I want to marry you." Sawyer sighed. "We truly care for each other, and the *kinner* are clearly as fond of you as you are of them. We're responsible adults who are old enough to know what we want and who try to obey *Gott*. And we're like-minded in the ways that matter most…especially in our beliefs about family and the Lord. You said these same things about Doris and John not two days ago!"

"I'm not talking about Doris and John. I'm talking about you and me," Hannah stated quietly, a note of resignation in her voice. "You mentioned caring for me. What you didn't mention—what you've *never* mentioned—is *love*. You once told me you thought love was a frivolity, not a necessity. I thought perhaps you were referring to the kind of romance teenagers engage in, but now I'm not so sure. Tell me, Sawyer, is love a necessity for marriage, or is it just a frivolity?"

Sawyer's head was swimming, and he felt as if he might keel over from the blistering heat. "What does it matter?" he asked with a sigh. "Your *groossdaadi* already irrevocably refused to allow it to happen."

"It matters," she said, straightening her posture and rapidly blinking droplets from her eyes as she beheld his face, "because even if my *groossdaadi* had said *jah*, I wouldn't marry a man who doesn't love me with his whole heart, the way I love him. I wouldn't marry a man who can't even say the words!"

"Hannah—" Sawyer began, but his voice was too raspy to be heard.

"I will honor my commitment to care for the *kinner* for the rest of the week," she said before walking away. "But you'll forgive me if I don't engage in idle small talk when you drop them off or pick them up."

She headed toward the school, and Sawyer stumbled back to the creek, where he dipped his hand to drink again and again, trying to fill what felt like an unquenchable thirst.

* * *

Hannah managed to make it through the afternoon without weeping in front of her class, but once home, she removed herself from the children's presence to blot her eyes. She keened forward and backward on her bed, willing herself to stop crying. It was one of her last days with Sarah, Samuel and Simon. She didn't want them to remember her as tearful and blotchy-faced.

There was a knock on the door.

"Hannah?" Sarah asked. "Would you brush my hair? Doris Hooley wanted to do it because she said I look unkempt, but I told her I wanted you to do it."

"Of course. Sit here beside me. You're getting old enough to brush the ends yourself now. Don't you remember the secret trick I showed you?"

"*Jah*, but *Daed* said we would be leaving soon, so I wanted to get in all the brushing with you I could," Sarah sniffed.

"Shh, shh," Hannah said. "If you fuss, you'll make me cry, too."

"If I write to you, will you write to me?"

"Jah."

"Can I come to visit?" Sarah pleaded.

Avoiding the question, Hannah corrected her, "*May* I come to visit?"

"Of course you may!" Sarah giggled gleefully until Hannah did, too.

But a few hours later, Hannah lay in the same spot, sobbing her heart out again. She hadn't cried that hard since her *groossmammi* died, or her parents before that.

She wondered if this was how Jacob Stolzfus felt when she told him she held only a sisterly affection for him. But this was different, wasn't it? She'd made it clear to Jacob on several occasions she was interested only in a friendship with him. Sawyer, however, asked her grandfather for her hand. He led her to believe he felt about her as she felt about him, didn't he?

As she wept, lightning flickered and the curtains danced as the breeze picked up. She raced to shut her windows. As the skies let loose a deluge of rain, Hannah wept a spate of tears, until another day dawned, hot and dry.

"You look miserable," her grandfather said when he finished his breakfast. "You're too old to be staying up half the night from a little lightning."

Hannah walked to the sink under the pretense of washing dishes.

"And *you're* too old to be making such unkind remarks!" she replied with her back turned, thrashing a dishcloth over the pots in the sink. "How dare you complain about what I look like? *You* have always tried to squelch every fragment of joy I've ever experienced. *You* are responsible for this frown I'm wearing, *Groossdaadi*. Because *you* have wanted me to wind up like *you*—a miserable, lonely, bitter old coot."

The combination of the scalding dishwater, her fiery temper and the broiling sun made her hotter than ever by the time she reached the stream. She removed her shoes to wade across, and as usual, the chilly current soothed both her mind and body.

Lord, please forgive my wrath, she prayed before continuing on her way. *Keep* Groossdaadi *safe this day. And if I should see Sawyer, please give me the grace to speak to him as I would want to be spoken to myself.*

When Sawyer came down for breakfast, he found Phillip alone at the kitchen table, drinking from a mug.

"Is that coffee or tea?" he asked.

"Coffee, of course," the teenager sneered, sounding

more like Jonas than like himself. "My *daed* is the only one who started drinking tea."

Sawyer poured himself a cup of the strong, dark brew. "*Jah*, tea's not for me, either. I wonder what other changes Doris will try to bring to this household."

"She can try to make as many changes as she wants," Phillip spit, "but she's not *my* wife and she's not *my mamm*, so I'm not required to do a thing she says."

Catching the resentment in his cousin's voice, Sawyer realized Phillip was only nine or ten when his mother died. Old enough to remember, but not necessarily old enough to comprehend.

He carefully suggested, "You know, your *daed* will never forget your *mamm* or the love they shared together."

"I know that," Phillip said with a snicker. "You don't have to talk to me like I'm a *bobbel*."

But Sawyer needed to speak what was on his mind for his own benefit as much as for Phillip's. "But your *mamm's* no longer here, and whether your *daed* remarries or not, nothing will bring her back."

Phillip rose and poured his coffee in the sink, but he didn't leave the room.

"No one will ever replace your *mamm*, not in your eyes, nor in your *daed's*. And I don't think Doris intends to try. In fact, I think it would be wrong to expect her to—even though I know she cares deeply about you and your brother, not unlike a mother might. But Doris and your *daed* have a unique relationship, one that's different from what your *mamm* and *daed* shared."

Phillip feigned a yawned, but he seemed significantly cheered.

"One more thing—you're right that you're not required to do what Doris wants you to do. But since you care about your *daed*, you should remember that he suffered unimaginable grief when your *mamm* died. If he's blessed enough to find a woman worthy of marrying again, you might consider honoring him by honoring that woman, too. And when you do, you shouldn't feel a bit guilty about it, because that's how your *mamm* would have wanted you to behave," Sawyer suggested.

After taking a swallow of coffee, he added, "Of course, that doesn't mean you need to start drinking tea."

"Jah, jah," Phillip agreed. "End of the lecture, Bishop Sawyer?"

"End of lecture. Now you go on ahead. I'll be out in a few minutes."

Sawyer pressed his palms against his eyelids, trying to block out the image of Hannah's pained face when he refused to say the words he knew she needed to hear. If only he'd had this conversation with Phillip earlier, he would have been more prepared to express himself to her. He knew his love for her to be true all along, he just didn't give it voice. He agonized that he was so inarticulate, always stuttering and stammering!

But what did it matter in the end? Her grandfather said he would never approve of their marriage. Hannah had to live with him for the rest of his life—it was better she should blame Sawyer for not loving her than to spend her daily life resenting her grandfather for forbidding their union. At least in time, Sawyer hoped she would forgive and forget him.

A shudder racked his body as he said aloud, "Even though I will never, ever forget her."

Chapter Fourteen

"The sky looks ominous. Would you and the *kinner* like a ride home?" Doris asked at the end of the day.

"*Denki*, but because of my absences, I need to catch up with my lessons," Hannah answered. "I've heard thunder growling all day, but so far, the clouds haven't erupted. If it begins to storm, we'll stay here until it passes."

After an hour of playing outdoors, the children traipsed into the classroom, sticky and panting from the heat.

"Will we have time to stop at the stream on the way home?" Samuel asked.

"I don't see why not," Hannah said. "As long as there's no lightning. Why don't you sit down and cool off for five minutes, and then I'll be ready to go. I'll even spoon the very last of my strawberry preserves from the jar for you to have on bread."

"Mmm," Sarah hummed after they'd been served. "It tastes just like pink sunshine, remember?"

"I remember."

"Why aren't you eating any, Hannah?" Simon noticed. "Are you terribly sick, too, like our *daed*?"

"What?" Hannah's ears perked up. "I just saw your *daed* drop you off this morning. What makes you think he's ill?"

"He told us on the way to school," Samuel said, hanging his head.

"Jah," Sarah confirmed. "He said he was terribly lovesick. That's what he said."

"Oh." Hannah gulped. She suddenly remembered what Grace had written about Sawyer being slow to express his affection, and her eyes moistened. *Was I too impatient with him, or did the* kinner *misunderstand something he told them?* "Do you know what *lovesick* means?"

"*Jah*, it means having a kind of sickness only grown-ups can get. *Daed* said it happens when you have love to give to a special grown-up but they don't want it anymore," Sarah answered.

Samuel added, "*Daed* told us love is like having too much strawberry ice cream. If you don't share it with someone else, if you keep it all inside, you get sick. You get lovesick."

"And since *Daed* has so much love inside, it's making him extra terribly lovesick," ended Simon.

"I see," Hannah said, crossing the room to the window so the children wouldn't see the tears escaping her eyes.

She blinked several times as she peered into the school yard, trying to clear her vision. Finally, she rubbed her eyes with her fingers and realized she wasn't imagining it—the distant sky actually was tinged with green. But there was no thunder. In fact, she'd never heard such silence. Not a leaf was stirring.

As if to challenge the notion, a tremendous gust abruptly lifted the branches of the willow tree and a cacophony of thunder reverberated overhead. The room went dim as instantly as if someone had doused a lamp and then just as suddenly was illuminated with a succession of brilliant flashes. Sarah screamed a piercing wail. Hannah barely had time to shut the windows against the barrage of hail bombarding the panes.

"Kumme!" she urged the children. "Under my desk, now!"

The children curled into balls on the floor, with Hannah shielding Sarah beneath her chest and the boys under each arm. *Please, Lord, shelter us with Your mighty strength. Please, Lord, shelter us with Your mighty strength*, Hannah prayed repeatedly as the atmosphere churned and cracked above them. The lightning was so scintillating and constant, Hannah could see it even as she squeezed her eyelids shut. The windowpanes popped like gunshot, and the force of the gale caused the desk to rattle like a train. Hannah tightened her grasp around the children.

"Hold on!" Although she was just inches from their ears, she had to shout to be heard over the ruckus. "Hold on tight!"

Such tremendous claps and clatters filled the air, she couldn't discern what was happening inside the schoolhouse and what was happening outside it. In fact, she didn't know if there *was* an inside anymore—it sounded as if the walls and roof had been fractured clear away from the building. Hannah tucked her chin to her chest against the dust and debris the wind was sweeping toward them in every direction.

There was a formidable splintering before *wham!*—something above boomed so forcefully that Hannah felt the floorboards jump before she and the children were engulfed in complete darkness.

Sawyer, John and the boys made it to the house just as the squall broke out, large pellets of hail bouncing off the grass as they ran.

"This is twister weather," John said breathlessly to Doris, who was in the middle of supper preparations. "The animals knew it before we did. I had a hard time getting your horse into the stable, but eventually he settled down."

"You're soaked, poor things," she said, handing them each a towel. A bolt of lightning cracked nearby, causing her to leap. "My, my. I'm not even afraid of storms, and this one is making me jittery. I hope Hannah isn't too nervous alone at school."

"You think Hannah and the *kinner* are still at the schoolhouse?" Sawyer asked in consternation. "Wouldn't they have left a long time ago?"

"I can't be certain," Doris stated, her pale skin fading to a lustrous shade of white, "but she had lessons to prepare. She said if a storm arose, they'd wait it out there."

"I have to make sure they're alright."

"Sawyer," John protested, grabbing his arm, "you can't go out in this. The horses are already spooked and will run off the road. The Lord will keep Hannah and the *kinner* safe. We'll go when it lets up."

"Neh," argued Sawyer. "I have to get to them now."

"I'll go with you," Jonas volunteered.

"Me, too," said Phillip. "*Daed*, you should stay here and make Doris a cup of tea. It looks like her nerves are frazzled."

By the time they'd hitched the horse to the buggy and set out for the schoolhouse, the storm had traveled at a good clip from the southwest to the northeast. They witnessed lightning forking from the bruised clouds to the horizon, but the sky overhead was already brightening. Steam rose from the ground, and the air had a metallic smell. The fields were blanketed in hail like snow.

As they neared the school, Sawyer was sickened by the sight of the damage: trees were uprooted and toppled, fences smashed and strewn, and a cow lay on its side in a field. He was grateful Jonas had the foresight to bring a couple of pairs of handsaws; more than once he and Phillip had to hop down and clear a path through the fallen trees. Sawyer realized this part of the town was the hardest hit. But nothing could have prepared him for the shock of seeing the schoolhouse.

One side—the side where Doris held her classes—remained relatively unscathed. Hannah's side, however, was nothing more than a heap of rubble, pulverized by the weight of the giant willow. Gasping in horror, Sawyer shouted, *"Neh!"*

When the noise finally abated, Hannah wiggled her fingers and her toes. In shock, she thought strangely, *I must be alive.*

"Sarah? Simon? Samuel?" She tried to call their names, but her mouth was dry.

The space was too tight for her to shift her body, and she was crouched in utter darkness. Nearly overcome by a wave of panic, she attempted to take a deep breath. It was then she felt the most marvelous movement beneath her chest, and subsequently each of her arms fluttered, too, reminding her of chicks hatching from their eggs. The children were stirring!

"Are you hurt? Are you hurt?" she repeated. "Wiggle your fingers and toes. Tell me if you are hurt."

When all three children confirmed they were fine, Hannah burst into prayer. "*Denki*, mighty Lord, for Your provision!" she sang. *"Denki, denki, denki!"*

"Is the storm over?" Sarah asked. "May we get out of here now?"

"It's very crowded," Simon whimpered.

"And dark," Samuel admitted.

"The storm *is* over," Hannah said carefully. "I know it's dark and crowded in here, but we'll get out soon. You see, the wind blew quite a few branches and pieces of wood down on top of us. As soon as your *daed* and the *leit* come, they will lift the debris up and we will climb out."

"Are we trapped?" Sarah asked, and Hannah could feel her body quiver.

"Trapped? *Neh*, we're *cozy*," Hannah replied. "This desk saved our lives! And do you know what? My *groossdaadi* made this desk many, many years ago when my *daed* was just a boy your age. My *daed* used to hide under it in the workshop. He pretended it was a cave."

"We can pretend it's a cave!" Samuel suggested.

"Jah," Hannah encouraged him. "When people are in caves, they like to pass the time by telling stories. Let's think back to the first day you came to school in Willow Creek and tell all of the stories we can remember about our time together."

"Like the time we caught the giant toad?" Simon asked.

"Or when we played that gold dust trick on *Daed*?" Samuel wondered.

"How about when we made snitz pies?" Sarah questioned.

"Oh, my," Hannah said. "Until this storm struck, I don't think there was ever a bigger mess than on the day we made snitz pies!"

"Jah," agreed Sarah. "Now, that was a real disaster!"

The four of them began to laugh so hard they shook.

"Hey! You're wiggling me like jelly!" Simon shouted, which made them laugh and wiggle all the more.

Sawyer had jumped from the buggy before he'd brought the horse to a complete halt. He sprinted up the stairs of the schoolhouse. The door to Hannah's classroom oddly stood standing, but the rest of the wall and roof were skeletal at best. The space once occupied by neat rows of desks was covered with thick willow tree branches, piled at least a dozen feet high. Fearing no one could have survived it, Sawyer retched at the sight of the destruction.

"Kumme," Jonas said, grasping his shoulder from behind. "They're not here. They probably left for her *grooss-daadi's* house before the storm broke."

Holding on to the possibility as a ray of hope, Sawyer turned to accompany his cousin when he heard it: giggling. He'd recognize the sound anywhere; it was the sound of his children's happiness. It was Hannah's wind-chime laughter.

"Hello! Hello!" he shouted frantically. "Are you there? Are you hurt?"

"We are here," a faint voice responded. "We're fine, but we can't get out!"

Tears sprang to Sawyer's eyes, and he didn't bother to brush them away as he scrambled over the willow branches. "Where are you? Call out again!"

"Under Hannah's desk!" came several voices in unison. "Front of the classroom!"

"We're coming!" he shouted back, using his loudest volume. "We hear you and we're coming!

"They're on the other side of this tree," Sawyer directed. "It's too high to cross. We have to come at it from the other side."

The back wall had collapsed forward, but Sawyer was able to determine the location of Hannah's desk by memory. He, Jonas and Phillip began heaving the wreckage over the side of the foundation to the ground below, assuring Hannah and the children as they worked that they'd have them out soon.

"Cover your heads," Sawyer yelled when all but the last layer of pilings had been removed. "Some of this wood might shift when we pull the desk away. On the count of three—"

Sawyer and Jonas tipped the desk at an angle so the foursome had room to escape. Samuel and Simon sprang to their feet, but Sarah's and Hannah's muscles were cramped from being in the same position for so long and the men had to help them stand.

After embracing his children in a tremendous bear hug, Sawyer instructed, "Jonas, grab the boys' hands. Phillip, you take Sarah. I've got Hannah."

His heart thudding like mad, he lifted her into his arms and placed her gently into the buggy. Her face was streaked with grime and her eyelashes were thick with dust, but he thought she was a most beautiful sight.

He asked again, "Are you sure everyone is unharmed?"

"We're fine," she confirmed, "but I must see if *Grooss-daadi* is alright."

As they charged toward her home, Hannah was appalled by the extent of the damage. Her stomach lurched several times, realizing her grandfather would never have heard the storm coming. She bit her lip and begged, *Please, Lord, let him be safe.*

When they crested the hill leading to her lane, her worst fears were realized: even from a distance she could see the chimney was all that remained standing of her house. The horse stall was smashed, as was her grandfather's workshop. The willow was stripped of its leaves, and the swing dangled like a flag of surrender from a top branch.

"Neh! Neh!" she moaned, scrambling over the children to leap from the buggy while it was still in motion. *"Neh!"*

"Hannah, wait!"

But Hannah ignored the voice. She ran to her grandfather's workshop and numbly began flinging pieces of wood from the pile. *A miserable, lonely, bitter old coot.* Those were the last words she'd spoken to him.

"Hannah, wait!" the voice said again, in her ear now.

Sawyer wrapped his arms around her waist and pulled her off the pile of debris, but as soon as he set her down, she bolted for the wreckage again. She had to get to her grandfather. He could be buried beneath the rubble, as she and the children had been. He wouldn't be able to hear her coming. She had to get to him. She had to let him know she was coming, that she'd never leave him.

This time, Sawyer restrained her arms as he embraced her from behind. She kicked him and wept hysterically. "Let me go! Let me go!" she yelled. "I have to get to my *groossdaadi*. Why aren't you helping me save him?"

"That's what I'm trying to tell you," Sawyer stated emphatically. "Your *groossdaadi* is alive. He returned in his buggy behind us just now. He said he was delivering a cradle to Miriam Stolzfus when the storm struck."

Sawyer loosened his grip on her, and she slowly shifted to see if he was telling the truth. Although it was dusk, there was no mistaking the stooped figure shuffling in her direction.

"Hannah!" her grandfather called. "My Hannah! I thought I'd lost you!"

Hannah's knees knocked, and her breathing was hard and fast. *"Groossdaadi,"* she whispered. Then the ground seemed to come up from behind to clock her in the head.

She woke in a room where she'd never been and shaded her eyes against the glare of white morning light.

"Hannah, it's me, Doris Hooley," a familiar voice greeted her. "You're at the Plank farm. You had a fall and bumped your head. It probably hurts and you may experience a bit of confusion for a few days, but you're going to be fine."

"My *groossdaadi*—"

"He is fine, although I must say he has a huge appetite. I think he ate four eggs for breakfast!" Doris chuckled. "The *kinner* are fine, too, to your credit."

"*Neh*, to the Lord's credit," Hannah murmured, suddenly flooded with fragments of recollection about what happened the day before.

"You may stay in bed, or if you can manage it, join us downstairs. I believe you're better suited for one of Amelia's dresses than for mine, so this morning I brought you one to wear. Sarah offered to brush your hair for you if I deem it *unkempt*," Doris said with a chuckle. "And the washbasin is freshly filled."

Hannah felt as if every bone in her body ached, and her mind was slightly addled, but she was so eager to see everyone, she dressed and hobbled downstairs.

"Guder mariye!" the children whispered.

"Doris said we have to be quiet because your head might hurt still. Does it, Hannah?" Simon asked.

"It hurts a little," she said, "but do you know what might make it feel much better?"

"If I fix you strawberry preserves on toast?" Sarah suggested.

"I was going to say *three hugs*, but now I think I'll say *three hugs and strawberry preserves on toast*!" she said, and the children readily complied.

"Hannah, *kumme*," her grandfather said from the porch.

He patted the swing and she sat down, positioning her body not only so he could read her lips, but so she could take a good look at him. She felt as if she never wanted to let him out of her sight again.

"Do you feel better?"

"Jah," she answered. "Much better. Safe and sound."

As the two of them sat watching the birds flit about

as if their world hadn't been turned upside down the day before, Sawyer ambled up the stairs and lowered himself into the spare chair.

"*Guder mariye*, Hannah," he greeted her. "We were all worried about you."

"*Guder mariye*, Sawyer. I am fine, *denki*."

"He wants to marry you," Hannah's grandfather announced in his characteristically bold manner, motioning his thumb toward Sawyer. "He has a *daadi haus*. I could work in his shop. You should consider saying *jah*."

Hannah closed her eyes. After all they'd just been through, her grandfather hadn't changed a bit. He still wanted to control her life, based on his own desires. Even more disappointing, Sawyer hadn't tried to convince her to marry him—her grandfather had done it on Sawyer's behalf, just like his children had told her how lovesick he was. Shouldn't these sentiments come from Sawyer? If he truly loved her, why didn't his words express what was in his heart?

"Neh," Hannah refused, and Sawyer's heart sank.

She squinted in her grandfather's direction, but her words were clearly intended for Sawyer. "You want me to marry him because our house and all that we own is gone, but even that's not reason enough for me, *Groossdaadi*. There are other things we can do. You can stay with Eve and Menno. I will live at Miriam and Jacob's and care for their *bobbel*. After that, we'll figure something out. The Lord will provide."

Her grandfather spryly leaped to his feet. He clasped Hannah's shoulder with one hand and Sawyer's with the other.

"I may be deaf, but nothing gets by me. I saw some time ago that the two of you love each other, and I was selfish to stand in your way. I didn't want to end up alone, but the *gut* Lord showed me yesterday how wrong I was to think I could hold on to you forever. For that, I am sorry, Hannah. I truly am."

Pausing, he took out a handkerchief and blew his nose.

"You are right. The Lord will provide our daily bread, whether or not you marry this man. If you don't want to marry him, don't marry him. That is your decision to make, not mine. You have my blessing either way," he said and then retreated into the house.

"Your *groossdaadi* is right," Sawyer said, leaning forward in his chair to brush a tendril of hair behind Hannah's ear. His voice was husky as he declared, "I do love you and I have loved you for some time. I just haven't expressed it aloud to you until now. I love you in a way I've never loved anyone before, and I always will."

Hannah's eyes, so soulful and blue, scrutinized his face. *She always seemed able to see right through me. She must know I'm telling the truth*, he thought.

Dropping to his knees, he pleaded as much as proposed, "Hannah Lantz, will you be my wife?"

Her eyes widened and she lifted her hands to the top of her head. Her lip began to quiver as tears streamed down her face, but she said nothing, neither turning away nor drawing near. His lungs began to burn, and he felt as if he couldn't get enough air. Unable to bear the silence, Sawyer closed his eyes. As he was wishing the ground would swallow him up, a butterfly alighted on his cheek.

Then he realized it wasn't the beating of a butterfly's wings against his skin; it was Hannah's eyelashes fluttering.

"Jah, jah," Hannah repeated, laughing and crying at once as she pressed her cheek against his. Sawyer wasn't certain whether she was delirious or ecstatic.

"Do you mean *jah*, you will marry me?" he asked, half question, half exclamation.

"*Jah*, I will marry you, Sawyer Plank," Hannah replied, nodding vigorously. "I love, love, love you!"

Standing, he picked her up, twirled her around, and then he kissed her softly on the lips once before setting her back on the ground.

With her brothers in tow, Sarah stepped out onto the porch at that moment carrying a plate of toast.

"*Daed*," she scolded, "you mustn't get too close to Hannah. That is how germs are spread. She'll catch your lovesickness."

"Neh," her father told her. "Hannah cured my lovesickness. I'm over it for *gut*!"

Epilogue

"*Denki* for hosting us this Christmas," Doris said as she cut slices of caramel pie for the adults to enjoy with their afternoon tea. "I've never been to Ohio before."

"I hope you'll come often. After all, we're family now." Hannah beamed. "Besides, it's the least we could do after you allowed us to get married at your home in November."

"Schnickelfritz!" Doris exclaimed. "Where else would you have wed? Where would your relatives have stayed? Your house was thoroughly destroyed."

"I suppose we could have gotten married next autumn, but we didn't want to wait a moment longer than we already had—we were following your example," Hannah teased back.

"You don't think I was being too *desperate*?" Doris asked.

"Neh," replied Hannah. "*Gott's* timing is perfect."

So were His provisions. As she prepared hot chocolate for the children, Hannah thought about how abundantly the Lord had provided for her, especially during the past autumn. John had allowed her grandfather to live in his home until he moved with Hannah to Ohio, and meanwhile he'd kept busy helping rebuild the schoolhouse.

Hannah had stayed with Miriam and Jacob, assisting their household as they ushered their healthy son into the world. Given the extenuating circumstances, the deacon had been very accommodating in meeting with Hannah and Sawyer as many times as necessary in order for them to marry in November.

Who would have thought the very kind of storm that was the source of so much loss and grief when Hannah was a child would ultimately result in so much gain and joy now that she was an adult? She sighed and filled the mugs as Gertrude scurried into the room.

"Oh, you've finished already! I was coming to help," the young woman said.

"You've already helped me in more ways than you know," Hannah replied, placing her hands on Gertrude's shoulders. "I've long meant to say *denki* for the postscript you wrote me on Sarah's letter. The part about Sawyer not being quick to express his affection helped me when I was filled with doubt."

"I should say *denki*, as well. I sense your influence in some of the freedoms Sawyer has allowed me as of late."

Hannah smiled warmly, lifting the tray of mugs. "Speaking of my husband, I heard him call me a moment ago. I'd better go see what he wants."

She stopped at the threshold of the gathering room to behold the scene inside: her grandfather was using blocks to construct a trestle for the wooden trains he'd made Samuel and Simon for Christmas. Their cheeks were rosy from helping him clear a path in the snow from his *daadi haus* to their back porch, and now the trio worked together in wordless cooperation.

"Make sure your railroad tracks don't run through my yard, please," Sarah requested from where she was seated on the floor nearby. She fingered the miniature table Hannah's grandfather carved for the dollhouse he'd presented her the day after Christmas, when the Amish traditionally exchanged small gifts.

The best gift I've received is to have all these loved ones in my family, Hannah marveled as she scanned the room.

"*Kumme*, sit with me." Sawyer gestured to the empty spot on the love seat after he had taken her tray and set it on a side table, which was modestly decorated with an evergreen centerpiece and candles. "We didn't want to start dessert without you."

"But first you must open the gift I brought," Eve insisted. "Here, Menno, could you please hold the *bobbel* while I give them their present?"

Eve deftly passed little Joshua to Menno, her face aglow.

"Motherhood certainly agrees with you, Eve," Hannah noticed.

"Funny you should say that," Eve replied as she handed her sister a large package wrapped in bright green paper and tied with silver ribbon. "Menno and I were just commenting to John and Doris how much we think motherhood agrees with *you*."

Hannah modestly dipped her head, but she was delighted to her core. When she lifted her chin again, she caught Sawyer's eyes sparkling with pride.

"It certainly does," he agreed.

"Aren't you going to open it?" Doris prompted.

Together, Hannah and Sawyer tore off the paper to discover the most beautiful wedding quilt Hannah had ever seen.

"Eve!" Hannah exclaimed, but she was too choked up to say anything more.

"All of my life, you've been like a *mamm* to me," Eve said. "Now I get a small chance to be like a *mamm* to you—the quilt is something I imagine our *mamm* might have given you as part of your dowry."

"But how could you have made it so quickly, especially with a new *bobbel* to care for?"

"I've been working on the quilt for years, Hannah," Eve explained. "I never stopped believing and praying that the Lord would provide you the desires of your heart, as well as your daily bread."

As Doris served the pie, Hannah interlaced her fingers with Sawyer's beneath the quilt and whispered, "Eve is right—through my new life with you and the *kinner*, *Gott* has provided both my daily bread and blessed me with the deepest desires of my heart."

"And our life with you," Sawyer murmured into her ear, "is sweeter than a dream."

* * * * *

Dear Reader,

Who knew, back when my parents first took my sisters and me on a long road trip through the Lancaster County countryside, that one day I'd end up writing Amish romance? I had no idea, although I was certainly intrigued by the beliefs and lifestyles of the Amish people we saw and met along the way. Sometimes, we just don't know where the road we're on will lead—both figuratively and literally speaking!

If you're anything like me (and Hannah and Sawyer), as you journey through life, you may find yourself concerned about your "daily bread." Likewise, you've undoubtedly experienced God's abundant and creative provisions, which were exactly what you needed when you needed them most. Including *love.*

Of course, no one makes actual "daily bread" quite like the Amish do, so if you're traveling through Lancaster County, be sure to buy a loaf—along with a sweet or two. Hannah would approve!

Blessings,
Carrie Lighte

SPECIAL EXCERPT FROM

Hoping to make his dream of owning a farm come true, Jeremiah Stoltzfus clashes with single mother Mercy Bamberger, who believes the land belongs to her. Mercy yearns to make the farm a haven for unwanted children. Can she and Jeremiah possibly find a future together?

Read on for a sneak preview of
AN AMISH ARRANGEMENT
by Jo Ann Brown,
available January 2018 from Love Inspired!

Jeremiah looked up to see a ladder wobbling. A dark-haired woman stood at the very top, her arms windmilling.

He leaped into the small room as she fell. After years of being tossed shocks of corn and hay bales, he caught her easily. He jumped out of the way, holding her to him as the ladder crashed to the linoleum floor.

"Are you okay?" he asked. His heart had slammed against his chest when he saw her teetering.

"I'm fine."

"Who are you?" he asked at the same time she did.

"I'm Jeremiah Stoltzfus," he answered. "You are…?"

"Mercy Bamberger."

"Bamberger? Like Rudy Bamberger?"

"Yes. Do you know my grandfather?"

Well, that explained who she was and why she was in the house.

"He invited me to come and look around."

She shook her head. “I don’t understand why.”

“Didn’t he tell you he’s selling me his farm?”

“No!”

“I’m sorry to take you by surprise,” he said gently, “but I’ll be closing the day after tomorrow.”

“Impossible! The farm’s not for sale.”

“Why don’t you get your *grossdawdi*, and we’ll settle this?”

“I can’t.”

“Why not?”

She blinked back sudden tears. “Because he’s dead.”

“Rudy is dead?”

“Yes. It was a massive heart attack. He was buried the day before yesterday.”

“I’m sorry,” Jeremiah said with sincerity.

“Grandpa Rudy told me the farm would be mine after he passed away.”

“Then why would he sign a purchase agreement with me?”

“But my grandfather died,” she whispered. “Doesn’t that change things?”

“I don’t know. I’m not sure what we should do,” he said.

“Me, either. However, you need to know I’m not going to relinquish my family’s farm to you or anyone else.”

“But—”

“We moved in a couple of days ago. We’re not giving it up.” She crossed her arms over her chest. “It’s our home.”

Love Inspired